LINCOLN AVENUE
CHICAGO STORIES

GREGG SHAPIRO: 77

Protection

LINCOLN AVENUE
CHICAGO STORIES

GREGG SHAPIRO

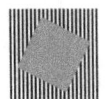

Squares & Rebels
Minneapolis, MN

ACKNOWLEDGMENTS

The author is grateful for the appearance of the following stories, some in slightly different versions, in these publications and anthologies:

BAC Street Journal: "Like Family."
Blithe House Quarterly: "The Breakdown Lane."
Christopher Street: "Lincoln Avenue" and "Swimming Lessons."
Jonathan: "Your Father's Car."
modern words: "Rocking Sylvia's World."
Mondo Marilyn (Richard Peabody and Lucinda Ebersole, editors; St. Martin's Press): "Marilyn, My Mother, Myself."

COPYRIGHT

Handtype Press, LLC
Squares & Rebels
PO Box 3941
Minneapolis, MN 55403-0941
squaresandrebels@gmail.com

Squares & Rebels, an imprint of Handtype Press, focuses on the LGBT experience in poetry, fiction, and creative nonfiction, preferably with a Midwestern connection. [squaresandrebels.com]

Printed in the United States of America
ISBN: 978-0-9798816-9-5
Library of Congress Control Number: 2014940300

A First Squares & Rebels Edition

in memoriam

Harry Shadrow (1913-2014)
Ilene "Lenie" Berg (1944-2014)
Leon Kaufmann (1936-2013)
and
Dusty (2001-2013)

Stories

YOUR FATHER'S CAR
I

THREES
6

LINCOLN AVENUE
20

LUNCH WITH A PORN STAR
28

DIRTY 30 AND TWO DOZEN
34

THE TRACKS
40

ROCKING SYLVIA'S WORLD
53

LIKE FAMILY
58

THE BREAKDOWN LANE
62

MARILYN, MY MOTHER, MYSELF
73

SWIMMING LESSONS
76

YOUR MOTHER'S CAR
83

YOUR FATHER'S CAR

You are driving your father's car, an orange 1975 AMC Hornet station wagon. The one with the black vinyl interior that gets so hot in the summer that your skin hurts just thinking about sitting in it or touching the steering wheel. And in the winter, the vinyl becomes so brittle that you are afraid to apply your full weight to the seats for fear of cracking them like ice chips. You are driving your father's car because your mother wears the key to her car, a lemon-yellow 1976 Lincoln Continental with a white vinyl top, around her neck on a gold chain, as if it was a religious medallion.

At first, it doesn't matter to you where you are driving, as long as it is away from your parents' house and the nightly dinnertime disagreements. Away from the eat-in kitchen with the lime green wallpaper, the sink with the coughing drain pipes, and the supermarket-purchased dinnerware, where the latest in a series of ongoing mealtime melees leaves you with the desire to join the Hare Krishnas, the Jews for Jesus, or any other cult who would have you.

Tonight's fracas is about the volume at which you play your stereo in your bedroom. Does it really matter that it is Barry Manilow's *Even Now* album? That most of your friends are blasting Led Zeppelin and Judas Priest and Black Sabbath from their speakers, while the fact that your record collection leans toward Manilow and Bette Midler, the 5th Dimension and the Carpenters is never even mentioned.

After storming away from the dinner table with all the delinquent drama you can muster, you throw yourself onto the lower bunk in the bedroom you share with your older brother and press your face into your pillow, wondering as you have before, how long you would have to stay in that position before you suffocate. But you don't want to give them the satisfaction of dying under their roof. You want to make them suffer. You want to go missing, end up hustling on the streets like Leigh McCloskey in *Alexander: The Other Side of Dawn*.

Initially, you stay close to home, driving a block over to Lee-Wright Park to see who is hanging out by the basketball courts. It's the usual collection of stoner jocks, perched on the back of the painted park bench with their Converse All-Starred feet firmly planted on the seat. Johnny and Scott and Bobby and Matthew in cut-offs of varying lengths and t-shirts exposing biceps and clinging to pectorals of different sizes. Johnny and Bobby are on the wrestling team, muscular and swift, and unbeknownst to the other, each has taken his turn wrestling with you. Not on the mat at the school gym, but on the carpeted floors of their bedrooms and later in their beds.

These are just a couple of the secrets you keep as you drive your father's car through the alley, and pull up behind the park bench and come to a stop. Scott looks over his shoulder at you and nods in acknowledgment. He runs track and field, and as he leans forward from his position on the park bench, his t-shirt rides up a little over his slim hips and you can see that he is still wearing his white Bike jockstrap under his shorts. You are familiar with the way it fits him, having helped him in and out of it on numerous occasions. Scott is fast, but you are faster.

Matthew's still mad at you about the hickey incident. He won't meet your eyes in the hall at school, and he won't meet them now. He doesn't understand passion or desire, abandon and free falling, the heat of the moment. He understands the pummel horse, the rings, the parallel bars, the trampoline. You understand the tramp part.

The four of them together like this floods your mouth with a salty taste. You look in the side-view mirror to make sure you are not drooling. After a few minutes, you pull away without saying anything and are surprised to see them each waving goodbye to you in the rearview mirror.

You push the last button on the radio and watch the red line slide to the end of the dial and come to a stop at WGCI. You turn on the radio, hoping to hear "Boogie Oogie Oogie" by A Taste of Honey, but you settle for "Macho Man" by the Village People. This music makes you think of the city and so you drive your father's car toward New Town, the intersection of Belmont and Broadway.

The fake ID Johnny made for you has gotten you into a few bars downtown, such as Alfie's and the Bistro, and also a couple in New Town, including the Broadway Limited and Center Stage. You've never told him where you go, and he's never asked. This arrangement has worked well for everyone concerned.

You are letting your father's car decide where you will go. It's a game you play, where you pretend the steering wheel is a planchette and the street is a Ouija board. You operate the gas pedal and the brakes, but you have no idea what your final destination will be. Tonight, as it turns out, it's the Glory Hole on Wells Street in Old Town. After a couple of swings around the block, you pull into a parking space a few doors from the entrance.

No sooner are you in the door, where the doorman glances at your fake ID with all the disinterest he can muster, than you feel several sets of eyes on you. You find a wall to lean against and reach into your back pocket for your cigarettes. You have only recently mastered smoking without coughing or getting sick. It feels like an accomplishment, like learning a foreign language or losing a few pounds on a diet.

You don't need to diet or put on a few pounds. You are, as most of the daddies in the Glory Hole would attest, just right. When you aren't slouching, you are easily six feet tall. You have a swimmer's build, even though you hate swimming. You have dirty blond hair, that you wear parted in the middle, slightly feathered. You have an unobtrusive nose, a strong chin and jawline, full lips, straight white teeth, and an attractive smile.

Your eyes are blue, but you've seen them cloud over and turn gray in the mirror when things don't go your way or you are deep in thought. Like tonight, when you stood before your reflection in the bathroom mirror, plotting your temporary exit from suburbia, knowing full well that it was futile to ask for permission to borrow your father's car.

After running through a few scenarios, one of which included dipping your hand into your father's pants pocket, while he took his post-feast nap on the couch in the den, you slip quietly out of the bathroom, out the back door of the house, and into the garage. Your father, who has locked his key in the car on more than one instance, keeps a spare in a magnetic case under the hood. You retrieve it, smooth as Robert Wagner as Alexander Mundy in *It Takes a Thief*, and make your stealthy retreat.

You light the cigarette and let it dangle from your lips, the smoke causing you to squint. You thrust your hands in the pockets of your new Calvin Klein jeans and try to strike a provocative pose. You are waiting for someone to come over and offer to buy you a drink. You don't wait long.

Knowing that you still have to drive your father's car to your next destination, whether it is to home or wherever the night takes you, you ask for a Perrier with a twist of lime. You make small talk with the man who buys you the bottle of fizzy water. It is hard to make out many details about him in the dimly lit bar. He could be anywhere between your age and death. He rests a hand, big and powerful, on your chest. You feel the warmth through the fabric of your t-shirt, which bears the name of your high school. You teeter between arousal and boredom. You think he may be slurring his words, at least the ones you can hear over the loud music. He leans in to kiss you in what seems like slow motion. You turn your head, and he licks your earlobe. You thank him for the drink and find another section of wall against which to position yourself for optimal viewing and display.

A man just a little taller than you slides over slightly to make room for you. You raise your green Perrier bottle as a sign of thanks. He raises his green bottle of Rolling Rock in a return salute. The next thing you know he is standing directly in front of you, looking into your eyes. You don't mind as he is much better looking, and maybe even less drunk, than the other guy. You move your mouth toward his but stop short of contact. He mimics you. You try to suppress a smile. He does the same. Your crotches meet. There is electricity. They stay pressed together like magnets and ball bearings. You imagine what your legs would look like resting on his shoulders.

When he tells you that he lives around the corner, the first and only thing he has said to you in the ten minutes that you have stood like this, groin to groin, you are grateful not to have to get in your father's car and drive anywhere. You wonder how you would have explained the orange Hornet to this man, to any man. You aren't even sure that you can still explain it to yourself. You dream of the day when the orange Hornet will lose its sting.

Little do you know that, in his spare time, your father has been trolling both the new and used lots of the local car dealerships. His list of complaints about the orange Hornet are much longer than yours, beginning with the way the car keeps running long after the motor has been switched off and the key removed from the ignition. The way the window on the passenger side has a mind of its own, rolling down whenever it feels like it, as if the invisible man is sitting in the passenger seat, the hand crank making its reverse spin to his unbelieving eyes. Not to mention how difficult it is roll it back up, as if the crank is a muscle man challenging your father to an arm wrestling match.

The eight-track tape player has the appetite of a ravenous piranha, the ceiling fabric sags enough to brush up against your father's bald scalp startling him on a regular basis, and the door handles, both inside and outside, are uncooperative. Little do you know that when your father finds a replacement, signs the papers, and plunks down the cash for his next car, the orange Hornet is destined to become yours.

THREES

Cliff had been unemployed for more than three months when he became convinced that he could conjure people by just thinking about them. The first time it happened he shrugged it off to coincidence and the fact that boredom mixed with no job prospects could do strange things to a person's psyche.

The second time it happened, he felt a chill that shook him to the bone and beyond. The third occurrence assured him that he had to make his strange new gift public knowledge. He waited a day in case there was another incident, but there wasn't. By Monday night, he was about to burst. He had to tell someone. So he called Jesse.

"Jesse," Cliff said with a half-chewed bar-b-q potato chip in his mouth, "the most bizarre thing is happening and I had to tell someone."

"What?" Jesse said. "What? Who is this? I can't understand you."

"Jesse, it's me," Cliff said, trying to swallow the sharp edges of the partially chewed chip and talk at the same time.

"'Me' who?" Jesse asked. "I know a lot of 'me's'."

"Me, Cliff," Cliff said, and something in his name made him start to choke.

"'Me, Cliff' should know better than to talk with his mouth full. Call me back after you've burped." Jesse hung up.

Cliff knew that sympathy was not one of Jesse's strengths. However, the ability to analyze dreams and other pseudo-psychic phenomenon was. After he drank some diet raspberry ginger ale and released a bookshelf-rattling belch, Cliff called him back.

"Did you brush your teeth?" Jesse asked, and without waiting for an answer said, "You didn't brush your teeth. I can smell sour-cream and onion seasoning all the way over here."

"They were mesquite," Cliff said, "and very high on the MSG scale. Is it hot in here, or is it just me?"

"Turn down the radiators and see," Jesse said.

"I was joking," Cliff said.

"So was I," Jesse said. "Now, where were we? You were saying something about a bazaar. We call them flea markets up in Wisconsin where I come from."

"No, not a bazaar. I said, something bizarre was going on. Weird shit. Very late-night cable TV. And I don't mean the Green Light Special on The Department Store Network, either. I mean, I think that I'm conjuring things."

"You mean like Samantha on *Bewitched?*"

"No. Well, yes. But more like Serena. I'm not conjuring *nice* things."

"Do you recite some little rhymed couplet first? Or do you just cross your arms and give a quick blink of your eyes?"

"Jeannie did the thing with her arms and eyes," Cliff said, frustrated. "Anyway, she wasn't a witch ... Oh, what am I talking about? Jesse, something weird is happening."

"Cliff, you think that if your mail is delivered later than 12:00 noon something weird is happening. You think that if Mary Hart is away from her *Entertainment Tonight* desk for more than two days that John Tesh is plotting to overthrow the show. How can I be sure this is genuinely strange? How do I know you're not exaggerating, something you and I both know you have a talent for."

"Look, Jesse," Cliff said, not angrily enough to make him hang up on him again. "I've suddenly been endowed with an unusual ability to make things happen and ..."

"So I should save the crack about your endowment until you've had your say, right?"

"Right! Jesse, in the last few days, all I had to do was think of someone or something, and they appeared or something related to what I was thinking happened."

"Start from the very beginning, because that's a very good place to start."

"Okay, Maria von Trapp, here goes. My dad sent me a clipping from the police blotter of my hometown newspaper. Apparently, this guy I grew up with was arrested for impersonating Jesus."

"I didn't know that that was against the law," Jesse cut in.

"Well, it is in Skokie, Illinois."

"Maybe you should consult with the Jesus impersonator," Jesse laughed. "He may have a better insight into your problem."

"Jesse, I'm consulting with you. Do you want me to finish this story or not?"

"Forgive me, Tabitha. Continue."

"Now, where was I . . . Oh yeah, the police blotter. They had this guy's age as 30. Now, I know we graduated from high school the same year, and I'm 32 . . ."

"You know, I've been meaning to talk to you about that, dearie. You needn't be so forthcoming about your age. I've been lying about mine for years."

"Yes, I know, Jesse. So does everyone you've been lying to. Anyway, as I was saying, I was certain that he was my age. I pulled my senior year yearbook down from the shelf, dusted it off, and found the faux-Jesus. I was right—we did graduate together. Since I had it open, I decided to flip through the pages, take a stroll down memory lane."

"Did you pack a lunch? It's a long walk."

Cliff ignored Jesse and continued his story. "Sometimes I play this game called Gay Match Game . . ."

Before he knew what hit him, Jesse started doing *The Match Game* theme song: "Da dada da dada da dada da dada da dada da dada da dadada, da da da da da . . ."

"Jesse, if you don't stop interrupting me, I'm going to conjure something to make you stop interrupting."

"Creepy Carrie! Creepy Carrie!"

"Jesse, do you want to hear the rest of this or not? I'm giving you the option."

"Well, I was watching the news since there's nothing else to watch, and *Melrose Place* is a rerun tonight . . . Okay, go ahead."

"Thank you. Where did I leave off?"

"Gay Matches. They don't burn, just singe a little. Oops, sorry."

"Right. Well, you'd think that in a graduating class of over 500, I'd run into one or twenty of my fellow classmates in Boystown. But no dice."

"That's because you went to public school, Blanche. All us future Baby Janes were busy fermenting in the hallowed halls of St. Bette of The Davis Catholic schools."

"Thank you for your input, Sister Jesse. So, I was leafing through the old yearbook, looking at the ridiculously posed senior portraits, lingering over the guys I remembered thinking were cute or hot back then, trying to guess who else turned out gay, and that was it. I closed it up, put it back, and went to sleep."

"Where does the conjuring part come in?"

"It's coming . . . Have a little patience. The next night, Saturday, I arranged to meet Lexie and Jade at Big Chicks. Lexie hadn't been there yet, and I'd taken Jade there for the first time the week before and, of course, she fell in love with the place."

"Must be the mammary menagerie mounted on the walls," Jesse alliterated.

"Jesse, it's art. Even though you're not a breast man, I'm sure you can appreciate an artist's rendering of the female body. You don't have to be a lesbian to enjoy the artwork on the walls at Big Chicks."

"But it helps. I mean, what would they think if I opened a bar called Big Dicks and the walls were hung with . . . Oh wait, the walls were hung, get it?"

With that, Jesse launched into a fit of phone-fumbling hysterics. Cliff figured that this was his only chance to continue, so he proceeded. At the rate the telling was going, he'd finish by midnight—of the next night.

"Harry White had also called me earlier in the evening to say that he might be stopping at the bar after a party he was going to in the neighborhood. I gave him the estimated time I was supposed to meet Lexie and Jade, and he said he'd probably be there around then. As soon as I hung up with Harry, I called Lexie. I wanted to warn her, in case she didn't feel like dealing with the 'Hairy White Man.' She said she didn't mind. In fact, she said she hoped she got drunk enough to haul off and deck him if he made one of his infamous misogynist comments.

"I got to the bar before Lexie, Jade or Harry. Being a Saturday night, it was packed, of course, but to make matters worse, the front end of the bar had been sectioned off for a birthday party. I stayed as close to the front as I could, not wanting to miss Lexie or Jade's entrance. I figured Harry would find me on his own; he always did. I think he's part bat.

"Sure enough, in walks Harry. He bellies up to the bar, orders a drink, and launches into one of his more idiotic spiels. From what I could make out, it had something to do with writing poetry under a pseudonym, an Asian woman's name, since according to Harry, magazine editors aren't interested in poetry by white men anymore. I kept casting sideways glances toward the door because I'd have to shut him up before Lexie arrived or she'd probably smash a beer bottle on the bar and slash his turkey-throat.

"Before I know it, he's ordering his second drink. A vodka gimlet, I think, and he downs it and orders a third. Thankfully, Lexie's hand is on my butt, her usual greeting, and I spin around to hug her and whisper a thanks in her ear for rescuing me. I hug Jade, too, but she's too busy checking out the art to notice."

"See, I told you," Jesse interrupted. "And those lesbians think we're perverse."

"Jesse, please. Between the jukebox and the birthday party, it felt like I was talking on a cellular phone that was really two beer mugs and a string. I lost count of how much Harry had been drinking, and before I know it, he's got one hand on my shoulder and he's trying to unbutton my fly with the other.

"I stopped him in the most polite way I could, and he announced that he was leaving. I didn't try and stop him, even though he was pretty blotto. When he got to the door of the bar, he turned around and bellowed in a voice that cut through the noise like an X-acto knife that he wasn't hurt by the fact that I had rejected his advances and that I shouldn't feel guilty if he died in a head-on collision on his way home to Logan Square."

"Hell hath no fury like a Logan Square queen scorned, is what I always say," Jesse interjected.

"Thank you for sharing some practical wisdom with me, Jesse. I'll have to remember that. Meanwhile, I'm getting some pretty strange looks from those around me. Lexie and Jade are doing their best to help me forget the embarrassment by making up a story about Harry White's funeral, after he does, in fact, die in a head-on collision with a bus full of Korean dry cleaners on their way to some meeting of the Rapture followers . . ."

"Hey, what's the deal with them anyway?" Jesse cut in again. "Do you think they're really in touch with all that because of the electronic equipment they manufacture? I mean, do you think Jesus is communicating with them via transistor? Maybe it's aliens; little green men who talk with an accent like Jackie Mason's."

Cliff was quiet on his end, actually stifling a laugh, because that could be construed as encouragement. Jesse noticed.

"Oh, I did it again, didn't I? Just as the story was getting interesting, too. I'm sorry. Continue, Cliff. I'll try to control my outbursts."

"Well, uh, okay, sure," he said.

"But don't take all night. I said interesting, not riveting."

"So," Cliff began again, "where was I . . . Oh, yeah, Harry White's funeral. Anyway, it's then that I suddenly realize that I really don't want Harry dead so much as I wish he'd just find another planet to inhabit. I say this to Lexie and Jade. And then I say it's Ron I want dead. Just like that, I say I want the man I spent 9.75 years of my life with dead. Through the haze of alcohol and cigarette smoke, Lexie and Jade lose their Hairy-White-Man's-Funeral glee and look at me kind of doe-eyed. So, then I have to qualify this by saying that it doesn't necessarily have to be a violent or painful end, but an end nevertheless. And I start feeling really dumb and hateful.

"I mean, we've lost so many close friends so quickly in the last few years, and I'm standing there wishing my ex-lover Ronny dead. But it's too late. I can't take it back. I've said it, and I've got to deal with it. And all of a sudden I get this weird feeling that Ron's going to walk through the door of the bar—"

"OH! MY! GOD!" Jesse bellowed. "You conjured Ron? How did he look? Is he still with that personal trainer guy? What was his name again? Earth? Moon?"

"Seed!" Cliff yelled so loudly into the mouthpiece that he hurt his own ear. "His name is Seed," he said, a little calmer, "and, yes, they're still together as far as I know."

This time it was Jesse's turn to go silent. Cliff thought he heard him whisper, "Go ahead," so he did. "Instead of Ronny walking through the door, Alec Silverman did. Alec Silverman is this guy I went to high school with. We were in a few classes together, but we mostly saw each other after school. Alec was one of the most talented singers/actors/dancers in the history of our now defunct high school. I was one of the most talented techies in the history of our still defunct high school.

"I, along with most of the student body, both male and female, had a mad crush on Alec Silverman. Unlike most of the student body, Alec and I were on a first-name basis. In fact, we were quite intimate at one time until Alec got stage fright for the first time in his career.

"I hadn't seen him since graduation. He went off to Juilliard or wherever it is singers/actors/dancers go to get a degree in singing/acting/dancing. I actually went to my ten-year class reunion on the off chance that he would be there. He wasn't, of course. He was in New York, in the chorus of some big Broadway musical.

"I felt foolish. Ron hadn't gone to his ten-year reunion, and I'd promised to take him to mine. Then at the last minute, I changed my mind, came up with some feeble excuse. All because I'd selfishly hoped to have just one more chance with Alec Silverman.

"I watched him approach us in the bar and then I turned my back on him. On Lexie and Jade, as well. They'd sobered up a bit since my pronouncement on Ron and noticed a change.

"What the heck, I thought, I was already down. I may as well tell them about Alec Silverman. And then I remembered looking at his senior portrait the night before in my yearbook. I looked at his picture the night before and there he was in the same bar as me on the next night.

"I told them this, as well as bits and pieces of the past. They both slipped an arm around my shoulders, one on either side of me. Just as I thought we were about to move into a much needed group hug, Lexie yells, 'Hey, Alec,' and once again, every eye in the bar was on us, including Alec's.

"'C'mere, Alec. There's someone who wants to talk to you.' I swear Jesse, all that slurring from Lexie, so out of character. I don't know if she was drunk on liquor or power.'"

"I warned you," Jesse said, adopting a parental tone, which irked Cliff coming from someone two years younger. "I saw it coming. But ya never did like taking my advice, now didya, Blanche."

"Jesse, I think I can handle myself where an occasionally overbearing lesbian is concerned."

"Dykes," Jesse countered. "Dykes on the cover of national newsmagazines and daily newspapers. In Gap ads and dishwashing liquid commercials. Lesbian chic will be the death of gay culture as we know it. Now, don't get me wrong. I have all of k. d. lang's CDs—even the one that's out of print—and I was a big fan of Kristy McNichol's when everyone else had given up on her. It's just that . . ."

"It's just that you're beginning to sound like Harry White," Cliff said, finally glad for the chance to cut in on Jesse. "I never noticed it before, but you do have the same condescending tone to your voice."

"Now, you've done it. Comparing me to that wretched old queen. I ought to hang up on you. But that's something Harry White would do, isn't it?"

Jesse sulked in silence on his end for about half a minute. "Oh, go ahead. Continue. That's just like you, Cliff, to insult me in the middle of a juicy story so I have to hang around for more details and potentially more insults."

Cliff imagined himself presenting Jesse with an Oscar statuette at the end of the story for his performance as best listener. "Alec wriggled his way through the crowded bar and stopped right in front of us.

"'Cliff?' Alec said. 'Is that Cliff? Oh, my God, Cliff, it is you.' The way he kept saying my name made me think about a line from *The Prime of Miss Jean Brodie*, where one of Miss Brodie's girls accuses Miss Brodie of always calling one of the other girls by both her first and last name because she simply couldn't remember who the girl was any other way.

"And I imagined as Alec was walking toward us, he was mentally going down a list of names before he got to mine and then that little spotlight went off over his head. *Bingo!* I tried to be nonchalant. My stomach was like a mosh pit. I was afraid that my tongue would be in a Boy Scout knot when it came time for me to speak. Lexie took care of that for me.

"'So, Alec,' she slurred at him as if it was the two of them who went way back, 'what are you doing here? Did you know that Cliff, over here, lives across the street in one of those renovated condos? Yep, he was one of the first tenants in the building, so he got to pick the nicest one. If you play your cards right, maybe he'll take you over there and you two can pick up where you left off. Know what I mean, know what I mean?' She kind of nudged him with her elbow when she said that. I was mortified, still unable to trust my mouth to speak. He smiled at me and instead of the usual effect those lips, those teeth had on me, I got strong. I wasn't about to melt like I used to.

"'What *are* you doing here?' I asked, feeling brazen and a little uncertain at the same time.

"'I'm in town to try out my new cabaret act before taking it back home to New York. I thought the folks in Chi-town might like a taste of what we're doing in the Big Apple.'

"'The way he said back home to New York, I thought how dare you speak in italics. And what person from New York actually refers to it as the 'Big Apple'? Probably the same person in Chicago who calls it Chi-town. I saw right through him. He was just as uncomfortable as I was, which I took great comfort in knowing.

"Jade, who had been silently taking it all in, spoke up. 'Lexie and I saw this cabaret performer at Michigan Moved, the womyn only performance space in Uptown. She was really good. She had big hooters, too.'

"Alec looked like he was drowning. I had to save him. Lexie and Jade meant well, but this reunion should never have occurred. I asked him where he was going to be performing and he said he would be at Le Bar, the new piano bar on Halsted Street. I told him we'd try to make it one night, and he said he'd put us on the guest list. He leaned in close to kiss me on the lips, I suppose, but ended up kissing the bridge of my nose because someone bumped him from behind. He said good night and walked away."

"You let him walk away? After your kind and concerned friends Lexie and Jade gave you the perfect opportunity to invite him back to your place? Which, may I remind you, is right across the street," Jesse said.

Cliff had to think fast. He wasn't really in the mood for one of Jesse's endless lectures on love and missed opportunities. "As if all this wasn't enough, Ron called me Saturday morning. He claims to have come across a book that doesn't belong to him and he thought it might be mine. Since the boytoy-in-residence only reads picture books, Ron assumed it wasn't his. He offered to drop it by my apartment since he was on his way out to run some errands. I assured him I would be in all day, doing housework.

"Just as I was about to hang up, he starts to tell me about this dream he had. When we were together, as you know, Ronny loved to bounce his dreams off me. As if I were a descendant of Freud or had any interest in Ron's dreams. I knew nothing about dreams, except that they occurred when you were asleep.

"So he proceeds to tell me about this dream he had the night before. He was having sex, of course, with a couple of different guys, one of which he says looked like me when we first met, young and thin, with a full head of hair.

"More guys enter the room in his dream and before you can say poppers, there's a full-fledged 70s-style orgy going on. One thing leads to another, and pretty soon Ronny had been lifted over the heads of the dream-orgy participants and he's being held aloft, sated, but still horny. In typical dream fashion, things change quickly, and he's being carried to a toilet-training contraption next to an open window. Instead of lowering and seating him, they throw him out of the window, where he falls and falls and falls until he wakes up.

"'If I would have hit the ground, I would have died,' Ronny says as a way of analyzing and punctuating the dream at the same time. All I could think to ask him was, 'What time did you have this dream?' Because you know how sometimes when you wake up from a really scary dream and you look around the room, trying to find a clock, so you can ground yourself in reality. What if the time was the same as when I wished him dead at Big Chicks? What if I wished him dead and he almost died?"

"What?" Jesse asked.

"I verbalized a death wish, and he almost died. In his sleep."

"You're serious, aren't you?" Jesse asked with genuine concern creeping into his voice. "Poor baby. Listen, I'm sure you're not the only one wishing him dead. He has a habit of making enemies."

"You think I'm making a big deal out of nothing?" Cliff asked.

"Well, they say that things happen in threes," Jesse said. "You know, deaths and other tragedies. Have there been other instances of conjuring since the last one?"

"Well, wait till you hear this," Cliff said. "I saw Cruella Corolla today."

Jesse thought for a second and remembered Cruella Corolla had been Cliff's nickname for his ex-boss.

"She was coming out of the video store in the mall at International Towers, probably returning an overdue genital-torture video. When she saw me, she turned positively peach. I just grinned, broad as the street, and didn't slow down my stride. I thought she was going to go into convulsions. Her eyes bugged out so wide, I was sure her glasses would fly off her face.

"She took a moment, composed the part of her visage that hadn't cracked and fallen onto the sidewalk, clutched her pathetic oversized Louis-Vuitton knockoff wallet to her skimpy bosom and almost tripped over her pigeon-toed self trying to get to her ten-year-old Japanese pseudo-luxury car, double-parked, of course, at the curb. It was my greatest triumph, and I didn't do a thing except think about her the day before. Eerie, isn't it?"

In fact, Cliff had been thinking about Cruella Corolla (née Carolina Seville) a lot during his extended period of unemployment. Cliff had been the Director of Client Services at International Language Labs until she canned him because he was looking for another job while he was still in her employ. He had thought he was doing a pretty good job of keeping it a secret from her, but he must have slipped up somewhere.One day, out of the blue, she called him into her office, which always stank from some exotic spice and cheap perfume. As usual, he was doing his best not to gag while talking to her in her cluttered cubbyhole. She was a gray-skinned Latina who always looked like she was in need of a good scrubbing and some roughing up by an oral hygienist.

She was the pride of her immigrant family, all of whom she had transplanted from Escanaba and 98th Streets on the city's far South Side to an entire floor of the International Towers condos in congested Edgewater. International Language Labs, in the mall level of International Towers, which she founded five years earlier, offered crash courses, taught by displaced persons, in foreign languages (none of which Cruella could speak fluently; for her, English still presented a challenge). The ridiculously overpriced classes were designed for the traveler on a tight schedule. Down the hall, and up a flight of stairs, on the mall's second floor, was the International Culinary Lab, another of Cruella's creations.

Apparently everyone who lived in the building, in the entire Edgewater neighborhood for that matter, had lots and lots of money to burn. Every class in every language offered in the I.L.L. catalog was filled to capacity. The cooking school, which had only been in existence for about ten months, was also a raging success.

Cruella proudly displayed her framed degrees of higher education in the reception area of I.L.L., where Cliff's desk was also situated. He was convinced that somewhere in her disaster area of an office were her real degrees: MBAs from every cutthroat business school in the country.

He'd been working there for almost a year when she announced a change in the benefits package. He was not happy about having been strung along. He had practically buried himself in debt anticipating his one-year anniversary and the big payoff. So he started scouring the Help Wanted ads. He had a few promising interviews before she caught on.

One of the interviews was arranged by his friend Russell. He called Cliff a few days after the interview to let him know that Cruella had slammed him, in broken English, to the director of Human Resources where he worked. He told Cliff he was really embarrassed since he had recommended him for the position. He was furious at him because he cost him his credibility as well as the nice referral check he would have gotten if Cliff had been hired.

Sabotage, Cliff thought. Cruella was trying in her lunatic way to assassinate his character. That really hurt since he was the one who singlehandedly reorganized her files and billing system after the guy before him quit without giving Cruella any advance notice. He had Jesse call her for a reference, too. She had apparently reloaded her weapon, leaving Cliff and his organizational skills bullet-ridden. On the day that he got up enough courage to confront her, she beat him to the punch. Since she couldn't fire him because he was looking for another job on his own time, she fired him due to a personality conflict. As far as he could tell, the only conflict was that he had a personality, and she didn't.

At the unemployment office, Cliff's caseworker presented him with a fax from Cruella disputing any and all of his claims. It preceded his appearance at the unemployment office by 24 hours. She must have been anticipating Cliff's next plan of action. He went over the list with Mrs. Katz of the Chicago Department of Employment Security, and they had a good laugh. It seems that Cruella was in the habit of hiring people and then letting them go around the time their employee benefits were scheduled to start.

Still, it was an awkward situation. She didn't want him to collect the unemployment benefits to which he was entitled (she did fire him, after all), and she wouldn't give him a decent reference so he could get a new job and get on with his life. What did she want him to do? he asked Mrs. Katz. Curl up and die?

Being unemployed was a terrible bore. After a while, the morning talk shows became a blur of big hair and regional accents. Oprah bleeding into Regis & Kathie Lee bleeding into Geraldo bleeding into Jenny Jones's leaking breast implants bleeding into Jerry Springer bleeding into Sally Jesse bleeding into Dr. Phil. However, Cliff was a trooper through it all.

All the free time was doing wonders for his already overactive imagination. He began plotting elaborate retaliation schemes against Cruella. Harmless pranks, really. She was in his thoughts constantly. Thankfully she never entered his dreams.

"Do you believe me now, Jesse?" Cliff asked. "I thought of Cruella Corolla, and there she was. I wished Ronny dead and he called me. I looked at a picture of Alec Silverman, who I hadn't seen in years, and he comes strolling in to Big Chicks. Is this a blessing or a curse?"

"I'd say it's a blessing, Cliff."

"Why's that, Jesse?"

"Well, we just happen to have an opening at the Psychic Sisters Network. Can you start tomorrow?"

LINCOLN AVENUE

This is Kenny's idea. He says, I'm gonna kidnap you. I say, who's driving. He says, you are. I say, how can you kidnap me if I'm driving? Like this, he says, and he makes a gun out of his thumb and index finger. Like this, he says and pokes his hand gun into my rib cage.

So, okay, I say, okay. Tomorrow, Kenny says, before I get a chance to ask, as if he knew I would. How much is the ransom? I ask, where's the note? No note, he says, no ransom. No ransom, I say and pretend to be insulted. No ransom, he says, unless you don't do what I want you to do.

Kenny's kind of cute, so I don't really mind. Tall and skinny, with curly blond hair. He's got this tight little dancer's butt, almost nonexistent. We're sitting in the IHOP at Howard and Western. I'm spinning the syrup tray, not really looking at Kenny. He's staring at me. Touch me, he says and I put my hand on his arm. He jumps as if I've startled him, as if I were filled with static electricity. This is what happens, Kenny says, this is how much I love you.

It really bothers Kenny that he can't drive. Dance or drive, Monica says. Monica is Kenny's mother, and she drives. When I'm not driving Kenny, she is. Kenny says, Monica drives me crazy, but you drive me wild. Baby, you can drive my car. That's our theme song.

Kenny puts his left foot up, on my side of the booth. Big feet, I say. So what, Kenny says. You know what they say, I say, about big feet. Yeah, Kenny says, big socks. Be serious, I say, or I won't put your big sock in my mouth. You wouldn't last two minutes without me, he says. He knows it isn't true. It's really the other way around.

I am one year, one month, and one day older than Kenny. He wrote the hours and minutes down somewhere, but I don't really care. All that matters is that I'm older. In my family, I'm the youngest of six, so it's nice to be older than someone. Kenny and I look nothing alike, so no one could ever mistake us for brothers.

What time do you get off work? Kenny asks. It's a silly question. He knows my schedule better than I do. The usual time, I say. I'll meet you by your car, he says. No, I say, make it interesting. What do you want me to do, he asks, hide in the back seat? In the trunk? How about under the hood, I say and give Kenny's foot a little squeeze. Ouch, he says, I'm sore. Madame Boris keep you on your toes too long? I ask with a twist of sarcasm. Kenny and I call his ballet teacher Madame Boris because he's an old Russian ballet queen. He's in love with me, but I don't dance.

Hitchhike, I say. Kenny says, what? Hitchhike where? On Dempster Street, by the entrance to the golf course, I say. Which direction, Kenny asks. Going east, I say, I'll stop and pick you up. What if something better comes along, Kenny asks. I blink at him. The smirk on his face freezes, then cracks. I'm not funny, he says, I was trying to be funny. You're funny, I say, what you said wasn't.

I blow bubbles in my Tab. Let's go, Kenny says. Let's not go straight home, I say, let's go the beach. I don't want to get sand in my shoes, Kenny says. We'll go Thursday, he says. I want you to get your rest tonight, he says, you have a big day tomorrow night. An adventure.

Kenny pays the waitress while I go take a leak. There's graffiti on the wall above the urinal. RUDY LOVES KENNY. MARIO LOVES KENNY. PAUL LOVES KENNY. I look down at the warm, yellow liquid spraying, splashing the cracked white urinal. FLUSH HARD IT'S A LONG WAY TO THE COKE MACHINE. BLONDIE SUCKS. RAMONES RULE. I hold my dick in my hand too long, feel it getting automatically hard. WHAT ARE YOU LAUGHING AT THE JOKE IS IN YOUR HAND.

I shake myself off, put it away, zip my fly. I flush hard, twice. And then, I see it, in red ink. KENNY LOVES ANDREW.

There are 137 notches on the black vinyl dashboard of my orange Dodge Dart (with the landau top), that we affectionately refer to as the Samurai Tomato. The notches are handjobs or blowjobs or an occasional penetration. Getting in is not important, Kenny says, getting off is. Kenny always takes a mouthful and kisses me before swallowing. I taste good on him like a secret recipe in the family for generations. You are living in me, Kenny says, I'll die without you.

Mostly we park in front of Kenny's house late, late at night. Monica doesn't wait up for Kenny. She knows I'm a good driver, she trusts me. The big song now is "Cars" by Gary Numan. It's our number two song. We sing along, sometimes add our own lyrics. "If Monica only knew/what we do do do/in cars." Monica knows, but she's not talking.

Kenny likes parks, too. Playgrounds with sandboxes, slides and merry-go-rounds. We like two parks best. Tecumseh Park, behind the bowling alley, and Carol Park, by the Rexall. We like them for different reasons. Tecumseh is dark, semi-secluded, with the back wall of the bowling alley on one side, a high fence and train tracks on another. One side faces Hull Street. The fourth side has a fence and bushes and an alley. Even though there aren't many trees, it's still easy not to be seen. Kenny carved our initials into the seesaw. K.L. + A.B. I lie very still on the seesaw, with my t-shirt up over my chest, my jeans down around my ankles, and Kenny teeter-totters me. When I'm upside down, Kenny gobbles me. I don't need drugs, Kenny says, I have you.

Carol Park is different. Surrounded by houses, businesses, traffic. We go there an hour or two before sunrise, sit in the submerged sandbox, leaning against the concrete walls. The sand is cool, damp when we arrive. Warm and sticky, when we leave. Once we startled an early morning businessman on his way to the train station. Two naked bodies, entwined at the bottom of the slide. Our clothes hanging over the swings.

On Wednesday, I have a bad day at work. My supervisor Jeff, who is married with two small mouths to feed, likes to follow me into the men's room, stand next to me at the urinal, and talk to my dick. Not to it exactly, more like at it, or me. He stands at the urinal, sometimes rubbing up against the off-white porcelain, both hands in his pockets, never opening his fly. Sometimes rocking back and forth. Sometimes standing still.

We talk about the teller line. Seven middle-aged women with overprocessed hair, and me. Once I asked him if having a bad dye job or an overgrown-out perm was essential for employment here at the Second National Bank. He just smiled stupidly and patted me on the head. He touches me, too. On the head, on the leg, on the back, on the arm, on the ass. Hands off, I say, I'm taken. Oh, yeah, Jeff says. Yeah, I say, and my boyfriend will kill you if you touch me. He blushes, quickly blanches.

Whenever I mention Kenny, Jeff goes pale. As if knowing about it and talking about it are two different things. They're not. So he brings the subject back to the teller line, where he feels safe, superior. We're gonna hire another teller, Jeff says, another guy, for balance. You'd have to hire three, I say, for true balance. One, he says, someone married, responsible, respectable. Oh, I say, wondering what I'd have to do to earn Jeff's respect short of coming in his mouth.

Dora, the head teller, is tapping her foot when I get back. Nervous, Dora, I ask. Yeah, she says, I'm worried about you, Andrew. Don't worry about me, I say, I can take care of myself. Dora has bad skin, and she looks like she's always flushed. One of these days, she says, I'm going to follow you into the men's room. That sounds like fun, I say, you bring the champagne, I'll bring the party hats.

When I get back to my window, there is a message from Kenny. There's been a change in plans. He wants me to meet him in front of Happy Foods on Oakton Street.

At 3:15, I punch the time clock and I'm out the door, quick as air. I'm wearing Levis, Kenny's favorite pair, the ones he says make my ass look like his. Impossible, I say, your ass is a work of art. It took years of fine-tuning and torture to get your ass to look like that, I say. Kenny looks right through me, clear through to the other side. His hand reaches around to where his eyes already are. He puts that hand into my back right pocket. Priceless, he says, and mine all mine.

Jeff watches me change out of my work clothes. Someday, he says, I'm gonna take you home to meet my wife. No thanks, I say, I don't do threeways. And I definitely don't do women.

Especially not older women. Jeff gets mad for the first time all day. Older, he says, she's only 26. He runs a hand through his hair. I'm certain that I see some gray hairs, but I don't say anything. Deep down, I think, I like Jeff and all the attention he gives me. Not that I'm starved or anything, Kenny gives me all I need and more. Someday, I think, I'll introduce Jeff to Kenny. Then stand back and watch them kill each other.

So, of course Kenny's not standing in front of Happy Foods when I get there. He's not in front of Oakton Bakery or the jeweler's. Maybe he's in Alexander's Five and Ten, buying gum or water balloons or a postcard. Maybe he's at Baskin-Robbins or in the Pro Shop or trying on jeans at Raymond's. All of a sudden, I don't care. I'll go to the movies or to Record City. I'll go to Cathy's and get stoned. I'll park in front of his house and lay on the horn.

Then I see him across the street in the playground. Sitting in the old fire engine, propped up on cinder blocks. Once I told him I wanted to have sex with him in the fire engine. No, he said, not the fire engine. Why, I said, I think it would be hot. I laughed stupidly at my pun. Because, he said, fire engines save lives. No, I wanted to say, firemen save lives. But he looked so serious, as if he'd lost someone near and dear to him in a terrible blaze.

I park in the Happy Foods parking lot and cross the street. For a second, I think I see my mother drive by with two of my sisters. But they don't stop, and I stop long enough in the middle of the street for an old man in a gold '68 Impala to honk at me and raise his fist. I run to the curb, giving him the finger, wondering where my mother and sisters are going and why I wasn't invited.

There are little kids everywhere. Swinging, hanging upside down from the monkey bars, spinning, jumping off the merry-go-round and landing on their feet. Kenny is the only one on the fire truck. He is smoking a Lucky. Why, I ask him, if you must smoke, don't you smoke a cigarette with a filter. I offer him one of my Kools. I want to know I'm smoking when I smoke, he says. Kenny taught me how to smoke. I used to just fill up my cheeks with mentholated air, release it when I couldn't breathe. You're holding it wrong, he said and adjusted my fingers. He taught me how to talk with it dangling elegantly from my lips.

How to fill my lungs with something other than oxygen, blow smoke through my nose, French inhale. I enjoyed the burning sensation in my nostrils, the hairs singeing, dying, falling out. We gave up on smoke rings. Your mouth, he says, is meant for better things.

Mothers and babysitters sitting on park benches call to the children. One older kid in the playground is one thing. Two is something completely different. Don't worry about us, I think, we've already got what we came for. Kenny climbs down from the recently repainted red fire truck. It seems to be up high, even for someone his age and size. I wonder how little children manage to get up in the driver's seat. I remember sitting up there as a kid, my feet not touching the jammed gas pedal or brake.

When we get in the car, Kenny gives my thigh a squeeze. Oakton to Skokie Boulevard, he says, Skokie Boulevard to Lincoln Avenue. Left on Lincoln, he says, I'll tell you when to stop.

We ride for awhile with the radio off, the windows down. It's that funny time of day in midsummer. It could be any time. The traffic is heavy but moving. Where is everybody going, I ask Kenny. Where are they coming from, he answers. Coming or going. This is a game we sometimes play when we've heard every song on the radio at least twice, and there's enough light to still see other drivers, passengers.

Look at those cheeks, Kenny says, puffing his own out in mockery of the woman driving the Maverick next to us. Coming from the all-you-can eat buffet at China House, Kenny says. Going to scuba-diving lessons, I say. Maybe she's trying to break a record by holding her breath, I say. Maybe she cut a fart, Kenny says and leans out the window, pressing his lips to his arm, making farting noises. I look in the rearview mirror and see a car behind me with lights on top of it. Cops, I say, and Kenny bumps his head bringing it back in the car.

Ouch, Godammit, Kenny says, and I look in the rearview mirror again and realize it was a taxi, not a cop. I reach over to Kenny, to the spot just above his ear where he bumped his head. I pull him closer to me across the black vinyl seat to kiss him, to make it better. His hair smells like baby shampoo. No more tears.

Kenny turns on the radio. "Life During Wartime." Kenny knows all the words. "This ain't no fooling around," Kenny croons and slips a hand between my legs, between the seat and the seat of my jeans. His face is almost in front of mine. I pull over. We are on Lincoln Avenue, near the Ground Round, where the Howard Johnson's used to be.

Are we there yet, I ask. No, Kenny says, I told you I'd tell you when to stop. Why did you stop? Because, I say, your father was a better carpenter than glassmaker. Because, I say, only your motives are transparent. Suddenly I wish it was dark. That we were parked here or in the Ground Round parking lot on the corner of Lincoln and Pulaski. That cars were speeding past us and we're in the backseat, wearing only our white t-shirts, our white socks. That I was straddling Kenny, our faces almost close enough to kiss. That Kenny's hands are on my hips, on my ribs, on my throat. That he doesn't have to touch me there, that looking at him is all it takes.

Horns honk all at once. Two, three, five. It's still light outside, approaching peak rush hour. I put my foot on the brake, Kenny moves the gear shift into drive. I creep away from the curb, squeeze into the ever increasing flow of traffic.

If you're good, I mean, if you behave, Kenny says, I'll take you to the DQ for a Blizzard later. Almost as if on cue, my stomach does a half-growl as we pass the Bunny Hutch. The air is hot dog-salty. Couldn't we stop now, I ask without a trace of whine in my voice, even though I'm beginning to see hunger stars. Swirling on the windshield, they are drawing pictures of French fries and milk shakes. Constellations I never knew existed.

Kenny pulls a Hershey bar out of his pocket. Melted flat and gooey, he peels the paper and foil back, dips a finger into the chocolate mess. Open, he says and inserts his finger between my lips and teeth. I lick like a puppy, suck like a newborn. It is sweet and satisfying. More, I say, and this time he inserts two chocolate coated fingers. I push the gas pedal almost to the floor. Intersections disappear. We make every green light.

We approach the Motel Zone, a strip famous for hookers, hustlers, drag queens, and bizarre, gangland style murders. Kenny says, Slow down, it's time for roll call. And we begin: Rio, Patio, Stars, Tip Top. Riverside, I say. Villa, Kenny says.

And we alternate. Lincoln. Acres. Together we sing, O-Mi. Turn in to the 2600, Kenny says.

This is not part of the game and I stop the car even though the light is still green. What about the Apache and the Spa, I ask, confused at the change in the game. The Summit and the Diplomat and the E-Z Lay? The light turns yellow and cars speed up to pass us. I feel my face getting red as the stoplight. Kenny reaches across me, and without even touching me, he flicks on the left directional. When the light turns green, Kenny says, go.

My heart adds a beat, skips a few. The DON'T WALK sign flashes in rhythm with the clicking in my chest. Now, Kenny says. He puts a hand, meant to massage, in my lap, but it only startles and disturbs. I turn left and left again without ever straightening the wheel. Up the ramp into the parking lot to where it says REGISTRATION. This is fine, Kenny says and releases me. The car is still rolling slightly, but Kenny is already out, the door opened and closed.

He is talking to the old gray man behind the desk. I imagine he is telling the man that he needs a room for himself and his new bride. Just married today by a justice of the peace at City Hall. I slouch in my seat, making myself shrunken, almost translucent. The old man doesn't look my way. He slides the guest book to Kenny who is pulling a wad of cash out of his pocket, passing it across the counter. His hands are large and steady, defined. The old man's hands are arthritic claws, knobby and unreal.

The bags are in the trunk, Kenny says to the ancient clerk as he is leaving the office, room key in his hand and a liar's grin on his mouth. He cocks his head to the left, a signal for me to move over to the passenger side. He wants to drive the car across the parking lot to the room. He wants to put on a show. Suddenly I love him more than air for this. For being the man in my life, when we are really only boys. For keeping me guessing, never sure from one day to the next if he will be fire or water.

LUNCH WITH A PORN STAR

The first time I saw Billy Bigg was on the northbound Ravenswood el, and I did a double take. He got on at the Merchandise Mart and stood near the doors after they closed. I was reading a back issue of *Details*, skimming an article about the evolution of the downtown club scene in New York, and flipping through the ads. I was riding backwards and the seat next to me was empty.

A tall, young African-American woman slid in next to me, her long legs barely out of the aisle. She had three oversized shopping bags from Carson's, Lerner's, and Walgreens. I moved closer to the window and adjusted my knapsack balanced on my lap.

My eyes left the pages of the magazine, quickly taking in my seat mate and the other newly boarded passengers, when I saw him. It was midsummer and, of course, the air conditioning on the train was malfunctioning. At each stop, the train's motor cut off completely, then quickly started up again with a zipping grind. The air conditioning chugged on, but by the time we pulled out of the station, it had stopped abruptly as a sneeze.

When I looked at the magazine again, all I could see was Billy Bigg's face as if it had been burned onto my pupils. My head popped back up like a quickly inflated balloon, and there he was. Dressed in a sport jacket and tie, pleated pants; there was a leather portfolio in his right hand.

Since I'd never really seen him completely dressed before,

it was that face I recognized. The blond hair, closely cropped on the sides, no sideburns. It was bushy on top and in the back. Those cobalt blue eyes, separated by the bridge of a perfect Roman nose. Lips, soft and full. Teeth white as cotton. The cleft in his chiseled chin almost as substantial as the cleft between his well-developed pectorals. His broad shoulders straining against the natural fibers of his jacket. He wore black Weejuns, easily a size 12.

My mouth was suddenly dry, the piece of gum I'd been chewing disintegrating on my teeth. I readjusted the knapsack on my lap for comfort's sake. My seat mate, flipping over the cassette in her Walkman, the Bad Brains from what I could make out, seemed oblivious.

I swallowed, the gum passing between my tongue and the roof of my mouth, sliding down my throat. I began choking, panicking, imagining the piece of Doublemint going straight to my appendix; as a child, I'd been told that would happen. I coughed and gagged through the Sedgwick and Armitage stops. By the time we reached Fullerton, I managed to dislodge the gum and my breathing returned to normal. When I looked over to where Billy Bigg had been standing, he was gone.

There is a legend surrounding Billy Bigg. When his naked face and body began appearing in all-male porno magazines and movies, the story was that although he made movies in L.A. and New York, he actually lived at home with his parents in Chicago. At the time Billy Bigg's name was becoming as big as the rest of him.

I rented a few of his videos from an adult book store. He was very popular, and there must have been at least twenty movies bearing his name in either the title or the cast. His image graced the covers of almost all the magazines, either alone or with one or two other guys. He'd even begun to appear in the bisexual movies that were becoming the rage in 1986.

He was a perfect symbol for the times. Sexy, cornfed, confident. As safe sex practices began to be pumped into our awareness, he was nicknamed the Saint of Safe Sex. He did speaking engagements and fundraisers for various AIDS organizations and refused to appear in movies without a condom on his famous endowment.

A month and a half went by from the time that I first saw Billy Bigg that afternoon on the way home from work. For the first few weeks after, I kept watching for him. But he never reappeared.

At first, I was afraid to tell any of my friends. Oh, they'd say, there you go again. That was in reference to my addiction to pornography. I had joined Pornonymous upon my return to Chicago when I realized that I had lugged 15 banker boxes of pornography across the country. Pornonymous helped me through a rough period. Listening to the other sex junkies, I realized I wasn't the worst off by a long shot. There was a guy who declared bankruptcy after not being able to pay his phone or credit card bills due to extensive overuse of the 976 and 1-900 phone-sex lines. I was relieved not to be him.

I got up enough courage to tell my friends about the Billy Bigg sighting.

"You're imagining things," Rick said. "The withdrawal has been too much for you, and now you're seeing porno studs on the street."

"On the el," I said, "and it was him. You could eat a scoop of ice cream out of the cleft in his chin."

"Oh, great," Alex said, "now the food fantasies are beginning."

"Fine, go ahead, make fun. You'll see. I'll have my day."

"Yes," Tony said, "visiting day. At Dunning Mental Hospital. I wonder how Billy Bigg feels about making appearances in psych wards."

I mentioned it once, never mentioned it again, having learned my lesson.

Then I saw him again. I was on my lunch break at the fast food mall on Wabash. Linda and Cassie, two of the work-study students I shared an office with, asked me to bring them diet Cokes and stuffed potatoes from Mrs. Peel's. I was getting a slice of pizza and an egg roll for myself.

I was placing my order at the counter of Fast Fong's Chinese Cafe when he got in line next to me. It was the first time I ever smelled Obsession on someone and fully understood the meaning of the word. I turned my head and looked directly into his juicy blue eyes. He turned the corners of his mouth up into a smile unlike any I'd seen in an urban setting. It was real and professional at the same time; a jarring combination. I smiled back, and for a second I could swear that his teeth sparkled the way teeth do in cartoons.

We said "Hi" at the same time and laughed bashfully. Fanny Fong, the excruciatingly thin daughter of Fast, called the number for my order, and I paid for it with slightly shaky hands.

"Bye," we said at the same time, and I nearly collided with a Chicago policewoman as I turned for the exit.

Back at the office, I sat at my desk, unable to eat lunch, my stomach hollow and empty, but somehow full. I should've done this, I should've done that. What was I afraid of? Being proven right, that my fantasies were coming to life? That they were real and breathing and living in the same city that I was? One thing I knew for sure was that I would see him again. I was sure of it.

But I didn't see him the next day as I'd hoped, or the day after. It was Thursday, and I only had one more day to see him before the interminable weekend. I couldn't bear the thought of Saturday and Sunday. What if this was the weekend he'd decided to finally make that long-planned move to L.A. or to San Francisco with his lover, who is probably a big porn star or maybe the president and founding member of the exclusive Billy Bigg Fan Club? What if he was single and on the lookout for a lifetime companion? Someone genuine, not synthetic like so many of his co-stars were. Was Bigg his real last name?

I pulled out the Chicago White Pages. Nothing under Bigg, only Biggs. Maybe he had recently moved and was listed in 411, but not the phone book. I dialed and the phone rang five times before a directory assistance operator answered. I said the name, spelled it, but nothing showed up on her screen. I hung up without saying thank you.

The next day I ran over to the order counter of Fast Fong's three blocks away. I tried to catch my breath on the walk from the front door to where Fanny Fong eagerly awaited her patrons. Most of the booths in the dining area were full. As I passed one of the booths for two, I heard someone say, "Hi, again."

"Hi," I said, looking toward where I had seen Billy Bigg a few days earlier. I had said hi without paying attention to the direction of where my words were going. People on a bustling downtown campus were always saying hi or hello or how's it going. No names; sometimes there were too many to remember. The reflex was to respond and move on. Classes to get to, conferences with instructors to attend. Then the voice in the booth said, "There's a seat here for you when you get back."

"Yeah, thanks," I said, my eyes scanning the crowd so intently for Billy Bigg that it took my ears a few seconds to connect the voice with the face I'd been looking for. I spun around quickly, just missing the same Chicago policewoman from earlier in the week.

"Watch it, pal," she said, "or I'm gonna take this personally."

"I'm really sorry," I said. "Don't arrest me, and it won't happen again."

"I was thinking more along the lines of writing you a ticket for reckless walking," she said and laughed good-naturedly.

I walked carefully to the front of the booth where Billy Bigg was seated, eating a fried chicken breast, and slid in across from him.

"This seat is for me?"

"It's yours if you want it," he said, wiping his mouth on a napkin imprinted with the logo for Pepper's Chicken Ranch.

"And you'll still be here when I get back with my lunch tray?"

"Right here," he said, "sitting across from you, like now."

"I'll be right back," I said.

"I know you will," he said, "Just look out for Officer Friendly."

And that's how I ended up having lunch with Billy Bigg. When we officially introduced ourselves, he used another name. While I was standing in line, a million questions went through my mind. Was he available? Would I have to pay for his time? Was he still making movies? Who was in charge of his wardrobe?

I looked at the people around me. Secretaries and students, lawyers and elevator operators. Everyone so busy trying to lead one life, let alone juggle two. A man I'd seen do remarkable sex acts on my VCR at home was sitting a few feet away, saving a seat for me in a booth lit by a single bulb in a hanging lamp. He wore a suit and tie, and he had big feet and hands. He probably worked in an office for some huge, impersonal corporation, where his coworkers had no idea what he did in his spare time.

Or maybe he had given it up, gone straight, so to speak. The obituaries in the papers were filled with the names and photographs of famous people, of regular people who were dying young or suddenly or after a long and tiring battle. Maybe he'd seen too much and decided to get out while the getting was still good.

In any event, I decided to let him steer the conversation. I looked around to see if anyone I knew saw me seated at the two-top with him. I tried not to stare, but he was a very good looking man, the most attractive man in the fast food mall, maybe the most beautiful man in Chicago. I wisely stopped at the napkin dispenser for extra paper products, worried that I might drool. Or worse. After all, it wasn't every day that I got to have lunch with my favorite porn star.

DIRTY 30 AND TWO DOZEN

Henry was one of the 25 people dressed like Riff-Raff, the butler in *The Rocky Horror Picture Show*. It was the five year anniversary of when the movie first opened at the Biograph; a Saturday night in April.

He was perfect for the part: tall and sinfully thin. His stringy hair went past his shoulders, long on the sides and in the back. He was mostly bald on top. He had false teeth after losing all of his own teeth to some exotic gum disease while a soldier in Vietnam. He usually removed his false teeth on request.

I knew Henry from when I was in college. He still worked in the bookstore there and sometimes as a disc jockey on the school's radio station. He flirted with me when I was a freshman, still a little wide-eyed in the city.

Once he organized a night out on the town for the theater majors. We had stuffed-pizza at Gino's and went to see *The Rocky Horror Picture Show* when it first opened in its midnight run. The theater was just half full. Only a few people talked back to the characters on the screen, and it startled me the first time I heard it.

At the time, most of us theater students were underage, but Henry knew of a bar on Rush Street where we could get in without being carded. There were seven of us, including Henry. The two girls declined the invitation as we walked toward Michigan Avenue. One of them had to be up early the next morning to sing in the choir at her church. They got into a cab and headed north.

At the bar, we huddled in the doorway where the bouncer was giving two black men a hard time. He said he wouldn't admit them without IDs. I looked at Henry who shook his head. The shaking meant two things at once. First, don't worry. Second, that racism was rampant in the Windy City.

Sometimes a memory consists of just smells, tastes, and sounds. Those seemed to be the only senses that I had working that night. The music was so loud that I gave up any hope of conversation with my friends. My skin was unaccustomed to the pulsing sensation of disco. I had goosebumps and the hair on my head seemed to be moving, too, as if the music was blowing it.

The bar was dark, but occasionally a face was lit up as it passed under the dim recessed lights in the ceiling, or the twirling strobe light over the small dance floor cast a flash in the right direction.

Each song segued into the next, and when one song in particular started, most of the men in the bar let out a yell and raced to the tiny wooden dance floor in the corner, packing themselves in tight as books on a shelf. It amazed me that so many men could fit into such a small space. They danced with abandon and joy, careful not to step over the boundary that separated the carpeting from the wood.

It was the first song I'd paid close attention to since we'd arrived and it seemed to go on for hours. "It's a shame," Evelyn "Champagne" King wailed in a husky voice while a bass and a drum encouraged her to continue, "a lowdown, dirty shame." When I hear that song now, I can't think of anything else but that night.

I also drank my first, and last, piña colada in that bar. Henry suggested I try one, thinking that it would be a good drink for an inexperienced drinker. The blend of tropical fruit juices and rum made my throat itch and my lips meet in a sweet pucker.

The air in the bar was heavy with the concoction of cigarette smoke, sweat and cologne. Not a bad smell, really; musky and potent. More intoxicating than any liquor. I was sure I would leave the bar with it clinging to me, like a lover until I washed it away.

Henry attached himself to Vincent that night. No one was surprised, really. Although, out of all of us, Vincent's sexuality appeared to be the most questionable. His beauty, however, was not. I think I was a little disappointed that it hadn't been me. But I was the one who became Henry's confidante through his stormy relationship with Vincent. And the next boy, and the next. I suppose I got the best part of the deal because I became Henry's friend.

This night, some years later, standing in front of the Biograph, I looked at Henry and thought of how grateful I was to know him.

"This is Colin," Marla said, "Henry's friend."

The weather was cool enough for a jacket or sweater. Almost everyone was in costume. Colin and I were the only ones dressed regularly. I liked him right away.

Henry held a joint in his mouth and lit it. After he took a lung-expanding drag from it, he offered it to me. I looked at it, then at Colin. His eyes seemed to say that he was waiting for me to make a move. Whatever I did was alright with him. I declined. Colin declined. We smiled at each other.

"I like your costume," Colin said without letting much time pass after our shared glances.

"I like yours, too," I said, "especially the eyes."

Marla shivered and pulled her frilly cardigan tighter across her shoulders. She was wearing an A-line mini-dress, pale tights and high-heeled Mary-Janes. She may have been dressed as Janet, but she was still very much Marla.

Behind me, I could hear music getting louder on approach. A boy in jeans and a t-shirt with the words SAY IT airbrushed on the front walked past, carrying a boombox. The volume was cranked way up so that the music and words to "The Time Warp" were a loud jumble.

"Turn it up," Marla said, "I can't hear it."

"Sit on my face," the SAY IT boy yelled.

"Table for three?" Marla said and chinned the boy.

We were quiet. Our mouths held between smirks and astonishment.

"Do you think his mother know he's here?" Colin asked.

"She is his mother," Henry said and cocked his head toward Marla.

"Yeah," Marla said, playing along, "he's just pissed because I won't let him breast-feed anymore."

Colin was looking at me. Was he waiting for me to jump in with a smart-ass comment? Did he want me to rescue him? What could I say that would be original and self-effacing at the same time?

"We're really not dressed for this party," I said, returning his look and then some.

I couldn't get past his eyes, dark as printer's ink. There was gray in his black hair, which could mean nothing. He was shy to smile, but when he did his teeth were white as envelopes and orthodontically straight. I wondered if he shaved before coming out tonight. There was no trace of beard shadow. I could have kissed him right there.

He held up the movie ticket in his hand as if to say, "What do I do with this?" I took it and offered his ticket and mine to Marla.

"Can you get rid of these?"

She opened her clutch purse and pulled out some money.

"I get a fee for scalping," she said.

"Whatever," I said, trying to move things along.

I wondered where we would go, how we would get there. I was nervous, which made me hungry. I could taste anticipation. We could walk to the Seminary Restaurant on the corner, or the other direction to the Salt and Pepper Diner. My feet wanted to move, to follow. I could ask Colin questions without fear of scrutiny. I had a list of other questions for Henry.

We stood around waiting for the right time to leave. I wondered if Colin had ever seen the movie, ever got up on stage, and jumped to the left. I ran out of fingers counting the times I'd thrown rice, toilet paper, playing cards and toast at the screen. Left the theater, hair wet, vowing not to return.

"Well, guys . . ." Marla said.

As if on cue, Colin moved closer to me. The tiny wrinkle lines at the corners of his eyes made me a little weak. I was 24, occasionally surprised by a pimple now and then. Most of the guys I was attracted to were older than me by a few years. Guys my age seemed dizzy and adolescent. I'd been living on my own for years, my parents waving me on as I pulled the packed U-Haul truck away from my childhood home.

Colin's past was a mystery. I wondered if we would sit in a dimly lit corner booth over coffee, trading pieces of our history like baseball cards. Never revealing too much, secrets like marbles in our mouths. If he was older, did he prey on younger guys as Henry did?

Nothing about him even smacked of similarity. He was preppy, where Henry was hippie-punk. Colin was clean, pleasantly scented, where Henry was indifferent. How long had they known each other? Since the war? Did they meet yesterday, during happy hour, Henry telling stories about me, his friend with the smooth ass and thick, curved cock, the words slurring into an invitation to a blind date?

"Which way?" Colin asked. "My car is parked on Halsted."

"I'm parked on Orchard," I said. "Let's just walk somewhere."

Marla moved forward to hug Colin. Her head came to his chest and she rested it there.

"Don't forget about my thirtieth birthday party," Marla said as a half-reminder, half-invitation. "Two weeks from tonight. I hope it will be as good as yours was."

"I don't remember much about mine," Colin said. "My Dirty Thirty blowout is a vodka blur."

"I have a few more pictures on the roll of film in my camera," Henry said. "When I get it developed, we'll show them to you. Maybe something will look familiar."

"When was your party?" I asked, feeling envious.

"About a month ago," Colin said. "If I'd known you then, I would have invited you. I needed all the friendly faces I could find."

"I would have come," I said.

An usher from the theater came out and said something about having the tickets out for collection. A man dressed as Frank N Furter, in ripped fish nets, fell to his knees and writhed on the ground at the usher's feet. I looked at Colin, and we both shrugged.

"Call me tomorrow," Henry said to me, "but not too early."

"Yeah," I said, knowing that he expected a full report.

Colin and I stood on the curb for a few minutes, watching the crowd, most of whom were dressed as Lina Wertmüller lookalike party guests, file into the lobby. A car drove by and honked, music blaring. I wondered if he liked to dance, to fuck or suck. Whether he listened to opera or Tom Waits. If he kept his eyes open when he kissed.

THE TRACKS

Cory Sparks stood on the corner of Niles Avenue and Mumford Street, smoking a cigarette. Early Sunday morning, three days before Christmas. The parking lot of the Christian Science Church was full. He could make out the sound of organ music, a choir, occasionally drowned out by a car speeding down Lincoln Avenue.

He walked to the corner, where Lincoln and Niles Avenues intersected, and looked south. The high school football field was now a parking lot. There was no trace of the Bays fast food stand that once stood with its neon donut balanced on one golden arch near the football field.

Looking north on Lincoln Avenue, he could see the junior high school with the bars on the windows. As students, he and his classmates used to joke about whether the bars were put up to keep them in, or out.

Just beyond the brown brick building, past the tavern and the gas station, was the senior citizens apartment complex where his mother's parents lived. He turned around and faced the old high school, now the home of a community college. "What happened?" he asked aloud, to no one in particular.

Cory flicked the cigarette into the intersection, dug his hands into the pockets of his leather jacket. He turned left in the direction of the public library, where Lincoln Avenue intersected with itself. Some of the houses on the other side of the street still had their Christmas lights on from the night before. Late sleepers, Cory thought. When he left home that morning, his mother was the only one awake. She was at the kitchen table, drinking coffee and reading the newspaper.

"Is that jacket warm enough?" she asked. "Don't you have a hat?"

"Yes and no," he said. "What time did you guys get in last night?"

"It was late, maybe 1:30. Aren't you cold, sleeping like that?"

Surprised, Cory looked at his mother. Had she come in to check on him when he was asleep, the way she had done when he was a child?

"No," he said, trying not to appear flustered.

"I know you've been living in a warmer climate, but I'm sure you haven't forgotten how cold it gets here."

"Winter in Washington gets pretty cold, too. It's not exactly Miami Beach."

"I was just asking, that's all. I'm your mother, I worry about you. It's a mother's right to worry. Is that okay with you?"

"Yes." He smiled, bent over and kissed her on the cheek. "I'll be gone for about an hour."

"Where are you going?"

"For a walk. Maybe over to see Gram and Gramp."

"Make sure you're back early enough to get to the airport. I'm sure your friend would be disappointed if you weren't there to meet him."

"Don't worry," Cory said.

"Take a hat," his mother said as he closed the door behind him.

When Cory got to the corner where the gas station was, he looked across the street at the building where his grandparents lived. It was relatively new, five years old at most, finished right after he moved to Washington. On his first trip home, he remembered driving past it on the way home from the airport. His parents told him about the waiting list of people trying to get into one of the low-income apartments. Somehow his father knew someone, had some pull in town, and was able to move his grandparents' names up higher on the list. Not high enough, however, and they had to wait three years to get an apartment.

From the street, he could see their kitchen light was on. His mother had told him that neither of them had been able to sleep through the night lately. This made Cory realize how old they were getting. He felt bad about living so far away, not being able to spend more time with his family. He looked at his watch. It was later than he thought. He decided to go home and call his grandparents when he got back from the airport.

As he walked up Lincoln Avenue toward Oakton Street, the heart of the downtown shopping district, he thought about the changes the stores and other businesses on the street had been through. His first job had been in a clothing store on this block. The once-thriving half-mile of stores and restaurants now resembled a ghost town. Lately, some stores that first opened their doors on the strip had closed and reopened in enclosed shopping malls in more affluent suburbs to the north. Some stores closed completely. Business was bad, and the merchants saw little chance for improvement. Shopping malls were tough competition.

Cory's mother used to teach first grade at one of the three elementary schools in their part of town. Enrollment had dropped and the school was closed. Two other schools in other parts of town were also closing. Young people simply weren't moving to this suburb and starting families the way Cory's parents had when they were first married. Cory remembered her telling him that she and his father had moved there from the city because it was such a nice place to start a life together.

One of the few things that remained from his childhood was the movie theater, next door to the senior citizen's apartment complex. It was still doing a booming business, even with the competition from the multi-screen movie theater near the town's shopping mall. It showed mostly second-run features and occasionally a Yiddish film festival. But at two dollars a ticket, the price was right and the popcorn was always fresh, topped with real butter. Cory remembered being dropped off with his sisters at the box office early on Saturday afternoons for the kiddie matinee.

While Cory, Sammi and Melanie were at the movies, their parents did the weekly grocery shopping at the Price &

Compare on Oakton Street. Cory looked forward to Saturday. His school friends usually met him under the marquee at the ticket booth or inside at the concession stand, and he sat with them, away from his sisters. It was in that movie theater with its sticky floors and velvet seats that Cory first thought he was different from other boys.

For as long as Cory could remember, the three of them would go to the matinee every Saturday. They would sit through cartoon shorts and the main feature, sometimes occupying the same three seats off the aisle in the center row. Cory loved the movies, which were usually Disney features, with an occasional MGM musical thrown in for variety. After they would see a musical, Cory would ask his parents to buy the movie soundtrack so that he could hear the songs again and again on the Motorola stereo in the living room. That was how Cory started a record collection that eventually included records by the Fifth Dimension, the Carpenters, Elton John, Barbra Streisand, and the Beatles. When a friend from school had lent him a copy of the *Woodstock* soundtrack and his parents heard Country Joe McDonald's "Fish Cheer" coming from the speakers on the stereo, they almost put an end to Cory's record collecting.

His sister Sammi was older than Cory by five years. While he was in the fourth grade at Edison School, she had already graduated from Lincoln Junior High and was a freshman at Niles West High School. She had strawberry blonde hair and green eyes and her body was filling out quickly. She was a cheerleader and president of the freshman class. The phone at their house never stopped ringing. It was either Mindy or Katie or Sari or Ellen. Boys started calling, too. Wrestlers and gymnasts and quarterbacks and first basemen. Steve called and Brett called and Ricky called and Dan called. Sammi talked to everyone, tying up the phone for hours. Finally their parents agreed to have a phone installed in Sammi's room with her own personal number.

At first Cory was a little jealous, but in the end it freed up the house phone so that he could use it without having to wait. Melanie, who was three years younger than Cory, didn't spend much time on the phone. She was content to play with her Barbie dolls and take ice skating lessons at the Skatium. Cory knew that this wouldn't last long, and soon the house would be filled with the sound of giggling girls on the phone.

When Sammi graduated from Junior High School that summer, Cory sensed a change in her that was subtle and unspoken, but there, nevertheless. She participated in family outings grudgingly as if they were an interruption in her busy social life. But the family routines never changed. Visits were paid to the homes of both sets of grandparents on weekend evenings.

Friday nights became Sammi's date nights. After much deliberation, their parents agreed to an 11:00 curfew. Sammi stuck to it unwillingly. Most of her friends didn't have to be home until midnight, if they had a curfew at all. On a few occasions, Sammi tried to test her parents' limits, once coming home as late as 11:45. What difference did it make what time she got home, she'd argue, as long as she got home safely?

From his second floor bedroom window, Cory sat waiting for the Camaros and Firebirds and Mustangs that Sammi's boyfriends drove to pull into the driveway. He watched the boys in their school letter jackets get out first and open her door. He thought it was kind of mushy but exciting, often wishing that he could be a part of it. The parties, the handholding, the walk to the front door, the good night kiss on the porch. Cory realized he envied Sammi. To be on the receiving end of the affections of one of the high school jocks made Cory's heart pound.

At the Saturday matinees, Cory observed Sammi and her girlfriends giggling and leaning on various members of the football, basketball, and tennis teams. The guys seemed to be all gangly limbs and grins. He imagined that they smelled like Brut or Old Spice with a hint of Herbal Essence shampoo.

He never told any of his friends what he was thinking. Never.

Cory had told Jeff, his lover of two years, everything about what it was like while he was growing up. Jeff was an only child. He had married, briefly right out of high school, and had a son because he was expected to produce an heir to the family's name. The whole time he was married he tried to repress his feelings of attraction toward other men. But since he had completed what he felt was his obligation to his family, he stayed married until his son was born.

Jeff and Cory met at an AIDS fundraiser in Washington, where they were both attending different universities. Both went there alone and ended up sitting at the same table during the dinner and speeches. By the end of the evening, they exchanged phone numbers. Jeff was a senior, majoring in business administration. Cory was a junior, majoring in theater arts with a concentration in directing.

Cory looked forward to introducing Jeff to his parents and sisters. Sammi was married to Phil, an accountant, and had a daughter named Vanessa. Melanie grew up to be very tall and pretty, prettier than Sammi. She lived in Austin, Texas with Brian who was the drummer in the band that Melanie sang with. There was talk about their band, The Utensils, signing with a major label after the first of the new year.

Three years earlier at Christmas Cory had chosen to come out to his family. Melanie had a different boyfriend at the time, and Sammi and Phil had just gotten engaged. The family had opened their gifts. They were watching the televised Midnight Mass. Everyone was quiet, listening to the cardinal speak, when Cory recognized one of the deacons on the pulpit. They had met at a party. He had gone home with him to his apartment in Evanston, and they had unremarkable sex.

Cory abruptly stood up. The hypocrisy and the holiday were too much for him to take. He began to gather the torn up wrapping paper from the floor and stuffed it into a big Hefty bag. After he was finished, he cleared his throat and said, "I have an announcement to make. I'm gay."

Everyone in the room looked at him for a few seconds. The silence was as heavy as the censer the cardinal was swinging on the television. Finally his mother spoke. "Cory, if you wanted help cleaning up, all you had to was ask."

After that, nothing changed. He was surprised and pleased that his family hadn't treated him any differently. He thought about how lucky he was that coming out had been so easy. Now, he was bringing a lover home for Christmas.

When he got back home from his walk, his mother was in the kitchen flipping through a cookbook. "Well, the menu is all set. Now you're sure Jeff isn't a vegetarian. If he is, I can make him something special."

"I'm sure, Mom."

"Really, it's no trouble. Remember the time Melanie invited her friend Dennis over for Christmas? She neglected to tell me that he was a macrobiotic. He drank bottled water that he brought with him in his knapsack for dinner. I felt so sorry for him. But what could I do?"

Cory walked over to her, sitting at the kitchen table and kissed her on top of the head. "No surprises from me, Mom," he said. "I promise." He took the car keys off the hook near the back door. "I'll be back in a little while."

"The tank is full. Drive carefully."

Jeff was the fourth person off the plane. Cory and Jeff embraced, and Cory took one of Jeff's suitcases to carry.

"I checked one bag. It's the one containing all the gifts."

"You shouldn't have," Cory said. "It really wasn't necessary."

"I wanted to make a good impression. How would it have looked if I'd shown up empty-handed?"

"It would have looked like you were a poor college student, which you are. Anyway, it's a nice gesture."

They walked through the terminal to the baggage carousels. Jeff told Cory about his visit with his family. He said that it went better than past visits, but it still left a lot to be desired. His son was getting bigger and talked a blue streak. His ex-wife was talking about getting remarried and seemed to be asking for his blessing. The whole time he was with his family he was thinking about being with Cory.

"I missed you terribly. How has your visit been going?"

"Fine," Cory said. "I've been catching up on some sleep."

"Speaking of sleep," Jeff said, "what are the sleeping arrangements at your parents' house?"

"We've been given the sleep-sofa in the family room."

"You mean we're sleeping in the same bed?"

"The operative word is 'sleep.' Although I don't know if I'll be able to control myself."

"Well, we could always give it the old college try."

When Cory and Jeff pulled into the driveway, Cory could see his mother standing in the big picture window. Her arms were folded, and she seemed to be staring into space, worry clouding her expression.

"I haven't seen that look since the days when Sammi first started dating," Cory said.

"What's that?" Jeff asked.

"My mother's in the window. She used to wait there like a sentinel until Sammi got home. Maybe she's a little nervous about me using the car. Well, let's not keep her waiting."

Cory briefly considered asking Jeff to wait in the car until he came around to open the door. He saw himself playing a part in the recreation of those Friday nights from long ago. But Jeff had already gotten out and was stretching his legs. The front door opened, and Cory's mother stepped out onto the porch and was walking down the stairs.

"You must be Jeff. I'm Sandy."

Cory was a little thrown by her first-name introduction.

"It's nice to meet you," Jeff said, extending a hand.

Cory released the trunk with the button inside the glove compartment and got out of the car.

"You guys missed all the excitement. Tony's mother, Mrs. Scolara, had a heart attack. There were paramedics and police cars."

"Is she all right?" Cory asked.

"I don't know," his mother said. "They rushed her to St. Francis. Tony had just gotten home, and he found her on the floor in the living room. What a terrible thing to happen right before Christmas."

Tony was one of Cory's best friends while he was growing up. They had known each other since kindergarten. Tony, and his mother, who was recently divorced, lived across the street from Cory and his family. As they got older, though, they began to drift apart. Tony hung around with a tougher crowd. He smoked cigarettes and dabbled in drugs. He got caught shoplifting, and his mother had him transferred from the public high school to a Catholic school.

It was cold outside, and Cory's mother wasn't wearing a jacket. Cory and Jeff carried the suitcases into the house. She stood at the edge of the driveway looking at the Scolara house across the street.

"Come on, Mom. It's cold," Cory said.

"I'm coming," she said as she turned around and walked toward the house. "I was just thinking about what a hard life she's had. That husband who used to hit her and that son with his problems. I guess I was very lucky to have three good kids."

She closed the door and hugged her son.

"We'll take the bags into the family room," Cory said.

"I left the sheets and pillow cases folded on the arm of the sofa. The pillows and blankets are on the top shelf of the closet in the utility room. If you need anything else, just ask. I've got to get back to the cooking."

"Thank you, Mrs. . . . Uh, Sandy," Jeff said.

"Yeah, thanks, Mom."

"Oh, don't mention it."

After she left the room, Cory and Jeff embraced again. Cory thought about how good it felt being in Jeff's arms, especially under the roof of his parents' house. Jeff kissed him on the mouth, and they parted.

"Well, do you want to take a nap?"

"Actually," Jeff said, "I was thinking about getting cleaned up and maybe going for a walk or a drive. I've been wanting to see for myself, all those places you've been telling me so much about."

"Oh, the grand tour," Cory said, "while it's still light out. This way to the lavatory."

While Jeff was in the bathroom, Cory thought about Tony. They had been so close while they were kids and then, after the incident at the tracks, their friendship quickly dissolved. He had told Jeff so much about himself, but he wasn't sure if he had told him about the truck. He would take Jeff there, show him the place where everything changed and tell him the story.

Cory and Jeff walked up Greenleaf Street alongside the synagogue.

"We used to come here and play hide-and-go seek. I don't think I'd ever been inside, but the outside had all these great hiding places. And then, of course, we used to ride our bicycles around the parking lot, crossing over into the big parking lot, over here at the train station."

Cory pointed to the parking lot on the other side of the fence that was owned by the Chicago Transit Authority. On the other side of the parking lot was the train platforms and the tracks.

"The trains that stop here go directly into the city. You have to change trains at Howard Station, but you can go downtown and beyond for one fare."

They walked to the low railing by the tracks.

"What's that other set of tracks over there?" Jeff asked.

"Those are the tracks for the freight trains. As children, we were forbidden to go near either set. Our parents warned us about the third rail and runaway trains. As far as they knew, we never went beyond our boundaries."

"Did you," Jeff asked, "go beyond your boundaries?"

"Oh, yes," Cory said. "Many times."

There had been an old, abandoned yellow milk truck left in the grass between both sets of tracks. Cory never thought much of it until one day when Tony told him that some older kids used it as their hideout. Cory asked Tony if he had been there, and Tony said, "Only once, when there was no one else around." He had seen guys going in there together. Sometimes a guy would bring a girl, but that didn't happen very often.

It was summer, and they were sitting on a park bench near the old field house at the park. Their bicycles were parked next to each other. Tony suggested that they take a ride over to the truck. Cory hesitated. A group of the older kids were playing basketball. "What if someone's there?" Cory asked.

Tony assured him that they didn't go there until later in the afternoon, usually after their game, since the days were longer and it didn't get dark until after eight. "Come on," Tony said, "there's nothing to be afraid of."

Tony stood up and went to his bicycle. He threw a leg over the seat and pushed the kickstand back with his heel. Tony and Cory were 11, but Tony looked older. He had grown two inches taller than Cory since last summer. His legs were long and lean and tanned in his cut-off jean shorts. He wore a black sleeveless t-shirt and his upper arms were smooth and slightly muscled.

Cory looked like his kid brother in his baggy madras shorts and striped t-shirt.

Cory got on his bicycle. He would wait until they were in the parking lot before deciding how far he would try to go with Tony. He tried not to think about how he felt about Tony. A feeling that was stronger than friendship. He was afraid he would lose Tony if he didn't follow him, at least part of the way.

The CTA train had just pulled out of the station when they got to the tracks. The parking lot was full of cars, but there were no people around. It was almost four o'clock. Tony leaned his bicycle against the railing and stepped up on the dull gray metal and over it. When his feet, in black Pumas, hit the gravel on the other side, it sounded like someone coughing. Cory turned around. There was no one there.

"Are you coming or not?" Tony asked.

Cory dismounted his bicycle and put the kickstand down. He followed Tony across the first set of tracks.

"Where's the third rail?" he asked.

"It's not where we are," Tony said, "and that's all that matters."

Cory listened for the sound of the crossing bells. He looked both ways before crossing the tracks as if they were some kind of unpredictable street. Tony was already at the truck, motioning for Cory to hurry up. The back doors of the truck had been torn off, and all that remained were the rusted hinges. Cory walked around the side of the truck. It said FRESH CITY DAIRY although most of the painted lettering had chipped and peeled off. The windshield was shattered, but still stood in place like crystallized spider webs. Cory walked around to the passenger side door, which was slid open, and Tony jumped out. Cory stepped back quickly, startled. Tony laughed and put his arm around Cory, leading him around to the back. There was an old, stained mattress on the floor of the truck. Piles of *Playboy* magazines were scattered everywhere. So this is what they do, Cory thought. Tony stepped up and inside first and extended a helping hand to Cory. The mattress smelled and was full of cigarette burns. Tony plopped down on the mattress and began leafing through the magazines.

"This is the life," he said.

He found a pack of Marlboros in a box and offered one to

Cory. Cory shook his head. Tony's dark hair was lit through a hole in the roof of the truck. He opened one of the magazines to the centerfold and said, "Isn't she beautiful?"

"No," Cory wanted to say. "You are." But he bit his lip instead.

Tony lit a cigarette with a butane lighter he had stolen from the top of his father's dresser.

The combination of smells overwhelmed Cory, and he felt a little dizzy. He sat down next to Tony.

"Hey, not so close," Tony said. "I need a little room."

Cory pushed the magazines aside. He looked at Tony, who was so enmeshed in Miss July, that he was oblivious to Cory's stare. Cory wanted to touch Tony, to kiss him the way he'd seen Sammi kiss Paul Berry. He reached over and touched Tony on the arm.

"Don't," Tony said. "What's wrong with you anyway?"

He kept his hand on Tony's arm until Tony pushed it away.

"Don't," Tony said. "I mean it." The cigarette fell out of his mouth and landed on the mattress.

Cory moved his face closer to Tony.

Tony backed away, and without warning, he punched Cory hard in the shoulder. "Get out," he said. "I knew I never should have brought you here."

Cory stayed put.

"If you don't leave, I will." Tony stood up. The cigarette smoldered on the mattress.

Cory said, "I'm sorry, Tony. I didn't mean to . . ."

"The guys were right about you," Tony said. "You are weird."

Cory was surprised and hurt. "The guys think I'm weird?"

"Yeah," Tony said, "and so do I." He kicked Cory in the rib cage, knocking the wind out of him.

Cory grabbed his side and moaned. He started to roll toward where the cigarette was burning.

"Look out," Tony said, and he pushed him out of the way. The mattress was smoking, and it made Cory choke.

"We've got to get out of here," Tony said, stamping around where the little fire had started. It was still burning.

He helped Cory out of the truck and across the tracks, and to the other side of the railing. A feather of smoke drifted out of the back of the truck. Cory had trouble breathing from the kick and the smoke. He leaned over the railing as Tony got on his bike.

"Not a word about this to anyone," he said. "If they thought I was responsible, they'd kill me. And they'd kill you too. We have to keep it a secret."

Tony turned away and pedaled back toward their houses. The smoke from the truck was getting thicker, black and cloudy. Cory straightened up as much as he could, but the pain was sharp. He got on his bicycle and went in the same direction as Tony. Instead of going home, he went to the park where the basketball game was just coming to an end. It was almost dinner time, and most of the players would be heading home. Cory walked his bicycle home as the sound of sirens filled the air.

"I think he was trying to destroy any evidence that we were ever there, that anything happened. A few days later he discovered that he'd lost his father's lighter. I found this out from a mutual friend. Tony never spoke to me again."

Jeff looked at Cory and then over in the direction of where the truck had been. "Do you think the police or fire department found it?"

"Maybe. But it was an accident. He didn't mean to set the truck on fire. Well, maybe he did."

The sky was losing its winter afternoon gray and easing into a cold, dark blue. Cory dug his hands deep into the pockets of his jacket. "I'm cold," he said. "Let's go home. We can continue the tour tomorrow."

Jeff put his arm around Cory's shoulder, and he leaned into him the way he had seen Sammi lean into Jim Harper. They walked home with the tracks, still as a dead snake, behind them.

ROCKING SYLVIA'S WORLD

Sylvia lunches with other Sylvias (none of whom are actually named Sylvia) from the North Shore. Girls from Chicago's West Side who reinvented themselves in Skokie, Morton Grove, and Lincolnwood, only to be propelled later by sheer luck and fortune to even better places: Northbrook, Highland Park, Deerfield, Buffalo Grove. Living in sprawling housing developments called Villa this, Casa that, and La di-da. The Sylvias from Wilmette and Winnetka, Glenview and Glencoe, look down their cosmetically altered noses at them. The ex-West Side girls don't care.

Sylvia winters in Florida. Tired of Miami and Fort Lauderdale, she was one of the first to buy property in Boca Raton. Other Sylvias followed, birds of a sequined feather, flocking together, getting behind the wheels of rented Lincolns to drive to Miami, to go slumming on Collins Avenue.

My father's money, which Sylvia calls her "second husband," pours like gold dust through her hands. Expensive foreign cars, exotic furs, tastefully gaudy jewelry, manicures, pedicures, massages, perms, and rinses. Plucks and tucks and waxing and whitening. Closets full of (eat your heart out, Imelda) shoes. Racks of beaded, sequined, hand-sewn, tailor-made, variable hemline, off-the-shoulder, strapless, backless, V-neck, A-line, little black, cocktail, casual, formal, this-old-thing, off-the-rack, out-of-date, back-in-vogue, last season, winter, spring, summer, and fall collection dresses.

Sylvia is my mother. I am Sylvia's son. Don't blame me.

I am her son in a black leather biker jacket, two pierced ears, 501s worn-at-the-crotch, a NO ONE KNOWS I'M GAY t-shirt, and a pink triangle tattoo on my right shoulder that she hasn't seen. Yet.

In Sylvia's world, no one is just gay. They either "go gay" or "went gay," as if it were as simple as choice. As if they chose going to Orlando over going to Boca. As if someone would choose a life of torment and tragedy, discrimination and hatred, instead of joining the rest of acceptable society. This one went gay, and that one went gay. Pretty soon the whole world will go gay. The whole world, that is, except Sylvia.

Dinner is her idea. We communicate best over dinner, especially when Daddy is out of town at the Kentucky Derby or in Las Vegas. She picks me up at the train station, a mile from my apartment, in her leased Lexus. She points out a new Cadillac parked around the corner from where she picks me up. I know that she and Daddy will be trading in the Lexus soon, feeling guilty about the economy. They are doing their part.

I suggest a favorite restaurant near the house. Only to discover that it has recently plummeted from her ten-best list. Lucky for us, Bruno's Pizza is nearby and on the way home.

After much debate, we decide on thin style, broccoli and black olive pizza with whole-wheat crust. We hand the unpleasant waitress our oversized menus. I pluck a pack of Dunhill Lights out of my pocket and slap them onto the center of the red-and-white-checked tablecloth. Sylvia winces.

"Oh," Sylvia says after the waitress has turned her slouched shoulders and started to walk away, "and a diet Coke with a wedge of lemon, please."

Sylvia takes her big, green, designer-framed reading glasses off and slips them into their expensive-looking case. She stands up without another word, which is my cue to join her, and we fill our clear glass plates with salad parts, then return to our booth in the nonsmoking section.

"Do you remember Chip Bloomberg?" Sylvia asks. A piece of spinach is dangling from her mouth.

"The star of Daddy's Little League team? Four years in a row? 'Blue Chip' Bloomberg? The kid with the built-in swimming pool with the slide in his backyard and the two ancient parents? No, I don't remember him."

"Well, anyway, he was dating Aunt Betty's niece, Joyce."

"Isn't he a little young for Joyce? The Chip Bloomberg I don't remember was only a year older than I am."

"So? Joyce just turned 41. That makes him only seven years younger. Not a big deal, if you ask me. Besides, all the men Joyce's age are duds."

"I take it Joyce hasn't resigned herself to spinsterhood yet? Good for her. So, how did they meet?"

"Chip's family is in the dry cleaning business just like Joyce's."

"Did you say Chip's family? Are his parents still alive? They must've been at least 80 years old when Chip was on Daddy's championship teams." (I exaggerate the *S*.)

"Well, then, they must be approaching 100 by now," Sylvia says, suddenly looking as if her grip on the conversation is slipping, anxiously looking around the empty restaurant for the waitress.

"How long have they been dating? Are they engaged? Were you and Daddy invited?"

Sylvia appears to be bracing herself for an eruption. "I need another trip to the salad bar. The pizza's taking too long." She makes a beeline for the modest salad bar.

My hunch is right. This dinner (her treat, of course) is chock full of gossip. I can feel it in the air over the nonexistent ambience. I wish there was a jukebox in the corner. I would stuff it full of quarters, so none of the bored waitstaff would be able to overhear our conversation. We are the only diners. We are in luck.

Sylvia is back with a leaf of romaine smothered in Thousand Island.

"Don't spoil your appetite," I say, spelling dirt and dish with my knife in the remaining creamy garlic dressing on my plate.

"How's your health?" Sylvia asks, stalling and playing Mommy. "Have you lost weight?"

"My health is fine, all the better for your asking. In fact, I've gained a few pounds. Winter does that to me."

"You were always such a skinny child," she tsks. "Too skinny. And you never exercised. I was jealous."

"I must have inherited your metabolism, Sylvia. You're still thin; you still have your figure. Your friends must be envious."

"Green as this lettuce," Sylvia says. Green is her favorite color.

We never even notice that the waitress has come and gone, leaving our pizza, steaming, in the center of the table. I slice and scoop a piece for Sylvia. I could swear her eyes are watering.

"I could go for a goat cheese pizza right now."

"It wasn't on the menu," I say. "Do you want to send this one back?"

She doesn't answer. She delicately cuts the slice of pizza as if it were filet mignon. "Don't forget to set your clocks forward," Sylvia says.

I take off my watch and move the hands forward, an hour.

"Not now," she says. "After midnight." She eyes the watch, a Cartier tank. "New watch?"

"A gift," I say, "from an admirer."

She bristles, which means that either the pizza is too hot or I've struck a nerve.

"A doctor." I don't tell her he's a Ph.D.

"So, Joyce isn't dating Chip anymore."

"Why not? Don't his parents approve?"

"Because Chip went gay."

I bite the inside of my mouth, which feels like the consistency of the pizza. I am feeling ravenous. I could eat the whole pizza by myself. I take the hot pepper shaker in one hand and the grated cheese dispenser in the other and begin sprinkling the pizza. Sylvia won't touch it now. Of course, neither will I.

"Look, Syl, I've seen Joyce. And if being gay weren't a genetic thing, I'd be the first to point to Joyce as a likely cause for homosexuality."

"I certainly hope so."

"What—that Joyce is a likely cause or that it's genetic?"

"Genes. Because I'd certainly hate to think that I had anything to do with it."

Negating the fact that Sylvia's genes certainly played a role in who I am, I prepare myself for the "I raised you and loved you and did everything the best I could" bit. I don't want to hear it. I want to hear about Chip.

"You know, I was reading that article in *The New York Times* and . . ."

"Good, Sylvia, you should read. Read everything you can get your hands on. I've got books. You want to borrow some of my books? It would be my pleasure to lend you some of my books."

It is quiet. It is too quiet. People walk by the window of the restaurant, and they don't look inside. I wonder if they know something about this place that we don't.

I take another slice of pizza and begin picking and scraping the crushed red pepper flakes off it. The inside of my mouth is throbbing. I look at my watch and subtract an hour.

"So," I say, breaking the silence like a piece of Sylvia's Swarovski crystal, "maybe I can go out with Chip. Would you mind asking Joyce to give him my number?"

LIKE FAMILY

Lily, your parents loved you. That's why they beat you with a paint stir, a skillet, a belt, clenched fists. That's why they bound your ankles and wrists with clothesline, your tights, kite string, your jump rope.

In our apartment below yours in the four-unit co-op that your parents owned on Greenleaf Street, we heard them drag you screaming one night into the bathroom. They left you there until morning sobbing into the tile floor, for being five years old, wetting the bed.

Did the other neighbors in the building, the unsociable Nelsons and elderly Bluesteins, hear you, too? There were things you didn't talk about in 1964, but some mothers on the block talked.

Do you remember the sandbox that your father constructed for us on the side of the building? He put it in the shade of a tree, in front of the row of lilac bushes that lined the alley. Do you recall how once he made us put our fingers on the ledge of the sandbox, while he danced a hammer around them, between them, because some sand had spilled onto the sidewalk?

We saw you and your parents in the hall, the night they put a cast on your arm. Your winter coat was hanging open, your good arm through one sleeve, and I could see your flowered pajamas. Your slippers were pink with bows near the toes.

You said you had tripped over your Barbie doll case. It's good that the three of you had time to get your stories straight in the car on the way home from St. Francis Hospital. But even then, you weren't safe.

I used to run inside the house when your father came home from work. I was afraid of his booming voice, the roar of his motorcycle, his suggestive tattoos. His basement workshop invaded my dreams. The tools, ominous as weapons, caught the light, and looked electrically charged and threatening. I dreaded the dark and dank one floor below our apartment, the shadowy sheds, the vocal furnace. It was a place in which it was easy to hide, but also easy to be found, to be cornered. But you knew that.

In the room I shared with my younger brother, I would sit by an air vent, listening and laughing quietly when your mother sang her pretend operas. It was hard to reconcile those sugary sounds, near perfect pitch laced with *la-la-la* and humming, with the woman whose moods could change as swiftly as the Chicago weather.

She thought nothing of interrupting our play time in the backyard or in your room with demands of silence, justifications for laughter. She would kick you without provocation, thought nothing of grabbing a handful of hair to bring you to your feet. Was I that unreliable a witness?

My father had a temper, too. It was always there poised under the surface, rising like red below the skin. All he had to do was raise his hand to send me flinching across a room; scuttling sideways, crab-like, for cover.

He had no qualms about spanking or slapping, grabbing an arm or a shoulder as if he didn't know his own strength. He had little tolerance for backtalk or disobedience. But he never broke or dislocated our bones. He never punched us or caused us to lose consciousness.

Family legend has it that I fell out of my buggy while he was buying gum and cigarettes on the way to the Laundromat in Albany Park before we moved north. I was just a baby, and he was a new father. But that was inexperience, not malice, not even neglect.

I never doubted that my parents loved me. They tousled my blond hair, never pulled it. My sleep wasn't interrupted by nightly raids. I regularly stood barefoot on top of my father's shoes, my hands in his, waltzed around the living room and into the kitchen to the strains of his favorites—Lionel Hampton and Count Basie.

At school, Lily, I was torn between ignoring you and taking you by the hand and running as far and fast, in any direction, as our feet could carry us. Teachers too involved in imparting the new math, American history, spelling and grammar, overlooked the telltale signs of bruised limbs and missing patches of hair.

Little by little, I revealed the source of the strange sounds emanating from over our heads. I was told that my imagination was too active, too vivid. I was accused of being a liar. I was reminded to mind my own business.

Here is a photograph; black and white, early sixties. We stood: you and me in the mammoth backyard of your parents' co-op. It must've been summer. My chest was bare, ribs prominent through the skin. Lilacs weren't on the bushes although there were leaves. I can almost smell the rhubarb growing in a corner of your mother's garden, the freshly cut grass.

We looked like siblings, our blond hair bleached white by the sun. We even had the same squint. We appeared to be happy to be in the radiant light of the Midwestern summer. But your smile is tentative, fragile. Your posture betrays you. You were only a year older than me, but it may as well have been ten years.

At night in bed, in the room below yours, securely tucked in, reminded that I was loved with nightly bedtime stories and good night kisses; I often wished that you were my sister. I'm glad that you weren't.

When my father's store on Larrabee Street in the heart of Cabrini-Green was looted and burned to the ground during the 1968 King riots, we came home to find that your irrational father, afraid that we wouldn't be able to make rent, had changed the locks on our front door. Most of our possessions had been tossed out the front window of our apartment scattered across the lawn. We moved away.

A few years later we moved back, one block south. By then, you and your parents had moved to a single family home in a not too distant part of town. Your name was rarely mentioned again by the gossiping mothers or the aimless neighborhood children. Then you died. I heard it announced over the loudspeaker at my high school.

You were in a psychiatric ward in an Uptown hospital overlooking Lake Michigan where you had been placed after running away from home on more than one occasion. They say you fell or jumped from your room on the eighth floor, a failed escape attempt. There was a broken window, bed sheets tied together into a makeshift ladder. Your parents weren't there, but I think they pushed you.

THE BREAKDOWN LANE

This is what I get. This is what I deserve. Pulled over on the shoulder of Lake Shore Drive in the 30-year-old sea-green Chevy II that my grandfather had been promising me since before I was old enough to drive. Turning the key in the ignition on the dashboard and getting weak, pathetic clicks. No sputtering, no hemming and hawing. Not even some secret code. Just clicks that sound like a cross between slipping dentures and a leaky faucet.

Where did I think I was going anyway? I'm pretty sure there are some maps in the glove compartment. Who am I fooling? I can't even fold them the right way, let alone read them. In addition to the twitch in my right eyelid, which has gotten progressively worse since I left the house this morning, I am map illiterate. I think I was absent from school a lot during the formative map skills part of my education.

I remember thinking they were spending too much time teaching us how to read maps. I had a theory, in fourth grade when the Vietnam War in full swing, that they were just preparing us to be soldiers, and that map reading was an essential part of going to war in another country. I was a peacenik, in bell bottoms and hand-me-down Beatle boots. All we needed was love, right?

I don't have to look in my wallet to know that my trial Triple A membership had expired, two years ago. It was one of the first pieces of car-related mail I got right after I inherited my grandfather's car. There must be some car owner's mailing list in circulation, passed from the gnarled claws of insurance salesmen to the grease-stained paws of mechanics. Somewhere in between are the manicured hands of car stereo and tinted glass and sunroof salesmen and their ilk.

Add a dead battery to the causes-of-death list. Wouldn't you know my grandfather had to have power windows? Not power steering or power brakes, mind you. I'm not complaining, but I haven't been to a gym in years, and I still have 40" biceps and a 36" chest and well-developed calves just from parallel parking and braking. The thing is, it's late July, at least 91 degrees out there, probably 101 degrees in here, and I can't crack a window.

No radio either. Not that there's anything to listen to on the AM dial, but it would have been nice to hear another voice beside my own inside this car. If I keep talking, I will drown out the voices in my head. Don't worry, the voices in my head are not telling me that I'm the son of God and that I should assassinate the first politician I see. I should be so lucky. The voices are doing a surprisingly good Oliver Hardy imitation, chanting, "Another fine mess you've gotten yourself into this time, Craig . . ." and so on.

If you asked me how I got here, I would probably shrug. I could blame someone else, but all you'd have to do is ask them and they would probably just shake their head in that way they do, knowing that I'm up to my old tricks even after I vowed to learn some new ones.

You see, it goes way back. Not discounting recent events that have unfolded like a garden of underwater man-eating plants. It's just that when you combine the past with the present and toss in the unfathomable future, well, you'd probably be sitting right here, next to me on the bench seat (reupholstered in my grandmother's old kitchen curtains). This car is old enough to be in the Smithsonian.

If pressed, I would say that things came to a head last week during a get-together at Ben's apartment. My friends took a vote and decided to tell me about it. None of them would look me in the eye. They kicked at the Persian rug, their shoes, their own shadows. They cleared their throats. They bumped into each other's shoulders, arms, backs, chests. If they kept this up they would soon be a mass of bruises and rawness.

"Would somebody please say something," I said, tired of being kept in suspense.

Ben pushed Lee toward me. Lee skidded on his heels the way cartoon characters do. He stopped inches from my face, eyes bulging in an expression verging on hysteria. He stayed that way, leaning into and away from me at the same time, his body curving like a road. Then he went slack, and he was the definition of droop. He'd never been sexier, even for a matter of seconds.

"We liked you better when you smoked," Lee said, a there-I-said-it smirk on his face as he regained his posture.

"I'm hurt," I said, really meaning it but pretending not to.

Allen was there to soothe the burn and make it worse at the same time.

"Craig, dear, we agonized over telling you. We all lost sleep, even me, and you know how important my sleep is. We couldn't stand the pressure of keeping something like this a secret. It was too much, like an aneurysm or something. One of us was bound to start hemorrhaging."

Was it my imagination, or was Allen biting back a smile? Were the insides of his lips and cheeks covered with fresh teethmarks? His eyes sparkled from some inner impish light, not from the halogen track lights of Ben and Lee's apartment. The light in Ben and Lee's eyes seemed to be as dim and flickering as a kerosene lamp in a hurricane.

"I'm hurt," I reiterated, "but I'm really glad you told me. You'll never know how much that meant to me. Never."

This is not what they really wanted to tell me. What they really wanted to tell me was that, even though they gave it their best effort, Ben and Lee were breaking up after three years and were in the process of finding separate living quarters. They wanted to tell me that even though we all knew it already, we were supposed to act surprised when Sunny and T.C. made their official announcement at dinner tonight about moving to Montana to open the world's largest womyn-only health retreat and gym.

They also wanted to tell me that I didn't deserve any more praise than Daniel, who was rocking quietly back and forth in the fetal position on Ben's bed in the next room for having quit smoking cold turkey versus wearing the nicotine patch, like

Daniel. When Daniel took to smoking and wearing the patch, he developed yellowish circles under his eyes and a slightly glazed, although not entirely unpleasant, glow around the gills. He looked like he just stepped out of a William S. Burroughs novel. I wondered if we, too, should take a vote before telling him.

The rocking had stopped, which meant the squeaking of the mattress springs had stopped, which meant that someone had better say or do something soon, because Allen could not tolerate lapses of silence. To Allen, silence was like a promise; only useful after it'd been broken.

"So," Allen half-said, half-sang in that way he had of breaking the ice and forming ice crystals at the same time. "Sunny and T.C. will be here any minute. They had to stop at the Womyn's Weigh health spa and drop off an extra set of keys because the night manager lost hers."

"Allen, why can't you say 'health club,' like the rest of us?" Lee asked.

"Because I find the 'club' connotation personally reprehensible. It makes it sound like unless you're a 'member,' you can't be in shape."

"Since when has exclusivity made you flinch?"

"Oh, gee," Allen said. "Look at the time. Let's put our claws away, boys and girls, and enjoy some nice cookies and battery acid."

"Battery acid?" Lee said. "Why, you're soaking in it."

The doorbell buzzed. I almost knocked Ben over trying to leave the carnage in the living room for the refuge of the long hallway where the buzzer was.

"After you," I said.

"No, go ahead, Craig," Ben said.

"No, really, it's your apartment. You buzz them in."

"I always buzz people in. Why don't you buzz them?"

"Why, thank you," I said. "That's mighty nice of you."

The doorbell buzzed again, and Daniel appeared in the doorway of Ben's bedroom, his hair standing up on end, his face a mass of pillow case creases, moaning softly. He sounded a little like the doorbell. Ben and I stopped in our tracks, our shoulders touching, pressed together in amazement like frightened Siamese twins.

"Daniel, is that you?" I did not recognize him at first.

"Daniel, honey, why don't you go back inside and lay down? We'll get the door. It's just T.C. and Sunny," Ben said in his most soothing social worker's voice.

"Or maybe it's the pizza." I suddenly remembered how hungry I was before we got sidetracked.

"Pizza?" Daniel echoed as if we were speaking in a foreign language.

Then he got this look on his face as if he understood what we were talking about, which changed into an "oh, my God, I've got the dry heaves" look, and he took off at a trot for the bathroom with his big, sexy hands over his mouth.

Even in the midst of psychic disorientation and physical discomfort, Daniel had the foresight and consideration to close the bathroom door. I could fall in love with Daniel if he wasn't such a casualty. As luck would have it, the group's only remaining intact couple and the pizza arrived at the same time. Leave it to lesbians to make an entrance.

"Why didn't we ever try to move into this neighborhood?" T.C. asked, plunking her motorcycle helmet down on Ben's leather sofa. "Parking is as abundant as pussy around here."

"Teese," Sunny said, although it came out more like 'sheeeesh.' "I wish you wouldn't talk like that. It puts the boys on edge. Not to mention sending a good crawl through my own skin."

"I'm sorry, Sunny-Bunny. It's just that it's like we've arrived at the intersection of Lesbian Lane and Dyke Drive."

"Forgive her, boys," Sunny said, slipping carefully out of her leather jacket so as not to break a nail. "Her helmet was on too tight."

Ben and I were paying for the pizza, trying to shoo the halfway-cute Middle Eastern delivery boy away before he started quoting from the Koran. We closed the door and took the oversized pizza box into the kitchen, both hoping not to cross Daniel's path, certain the aroma would be enough to send him lurching into the bathroom again.

While the breakup was still in the early stages, Ben and Lee had the kitchen remodeled, which still smelled a cross between construction and the pages of *House* Magazine. Ben gingerly set the pizza on top of the butcher block island/counter. He cleared his throat; part nervous habit, part conversation starter. I took his cue.

"I don't know how to ask this politely, so I'll just ask. Who's staying and who's going?"

Our eyes met for a second, and in that brief span of time, Ben's face ran the gamut from confusion to confession.

"Me" was all he said.

This was obviously not the time to discuss the situation. Ben acted as if his hands and arms were wrapped in gauze and I felt like the idiot who asked him whether they were broken or just sprained. He might have been missing parts for all I knew.

Small warm hands, smelling faintly of gasoline and mink oil, covered my eyes. "Guess who, Pumpkin," someone whispered in my ear.

Since Sunny was the only one who called me Pumpkin, I feigned ignorance. "Hillary Rodham Clinton? Melissa Rivers? Wrong? T.C., the perfect lesbian species? Sunny, sweet as honey?"

"God, I've missed you," Sunny said as her hands slid down my face to rest on my shoulders. She must have been standing on her tippy-toes to reach my eyes in the "Guess who?" position.

"Don't give him a complex," Allen said from the doorway of the kitchen. "Just call him Craig like everyone else."

"Oh, Allen, he is like a god to me. So big and strong and smart and self-assured."

"T.C.'s in the other room, Sunny," Allen said, straightening his cuffs. "How long have you been confusing the two of them?"

"Craig's one of my heroes. It's his amazing ability to bounce back in the face of adversity that gives me strength. After all, he did survive being your boyfriend, Allen. Didn't he?"

"And the scars have healed remarkably, too," Allen said. "Have you had work done?"

"Only up here," I said, tapping my temple.

Things went, shall we say, downhill from there. Ben looked around the kitchen to see if there were any sharp or blunt objects within our reach. Thankfully, there weren't. We retired to the living room. Pizza was served. Announcements were made. Real tears were shed. I got heartburn.

I kept waiting for someone to say it was all a joke, a tasteless prank. No such luck. There were things I wanted to say, but I felt myself teetering so close to the edge of the precipice, that I bit my lip instead and excused myself. I pulled down my pants and sat on the closed toilet seat and cried quietly into the roll of toilet paper.

That was almost a week ago. Or was it yesterday?

Did I mention that my watch died? You know, the one with the calendar. When you're as footloose as I am, what difference does the time and date make? Yeah, right. Try telling that to a bill collector. Which brings me to the final blow, the last resort (no vacancies), the plastic cherry on the cake.

You see, I owe my father a lot of money. Since I can't pay him back yesterday and his business continues on its downward spiral, the amount has taken on mythical proportions. Two thousand dollars, give or take a couple hundred, is really small potatoes when compared to my other debts.

Only death can erase my debts. Debts are what I dream about. Every night at approximately the same time, my eyes snap open from a variation on the same dream, and the numbers on my LED alarm clock are dollar signs until I blink them back into digits. My license plates say it all: IOEVRY1.

Here's an unedited list: a student loan (for a degree I never even earned), 15 maxed-out credit cards (count 'em), insurance policies (apartment, health and life), CD clubs, book clubs, magazine subscriptions, past-due rent, and utilities.

My father doesn't send past due notices when I'm late with a payment; just verbal reminders so utterly lacking in subtlety that to call them obvious would be just as utterly lacking in logic. If I wasn't so sure I was adopted, I would say that I got my timing and razor-sharp wit from him. My sense of humor came from my mother who really needed one to stay married to my father. Alas, wit and humor can't get the creditors off my back. It certainly doesn't prepare me for my father's collection agent act, which is going into an unlimited run anywhere there's an audience of at least one.

It usually happens whenever we drive past the convenience store in the strip mall on the Evanston side of Howard Street. The car fills with tension-fumes as deadly, as invisible, as odorless as carbon monoxide. I wonder if I am the only one who hears the hissing, sees the black rubber hose dangling snake-like from the driver's side window. No one is paying any attention. We are too busy trying to breathe. We don't run red lights, drive up on the sidewalk, or into the headlights of an oncoming car. We stay in our lane, maintain the speed limit. We are good at repressing. Still, I can't help but wonder what is being repressed.

My patience is rewarded. On an unseasonably cold Father's Day, I am blessed with knowledge.

"See that store?" My father, who has also recently become a grandfather courtesy of my younger brother and sister-in-law, asks.

How could I have missed it? I've been dreaming of "that store" for years. It doesn't matter what city, country or time zone I'm in or between; I'm dreaming of the Ice Box Convenience Store. Passing it going north, west, south, east, from above, below, this side of the street, that side, in slow motion, in time-lapse photography, in the morning, in the afternoon, after dark. No matter what time of day it is or if I'm travelling on foot or by car, I pass the big picture window of the Ice Box Convenience Store glowing like a downtown department store. I look in the window and see everything but my own reflection. It is the only dream I remember, the only one I want to forget.

"It's your bar mitzvah," my father says, playing with the tinted power windows. "Take a good look at it. That's your bar mitzvah."

I know what he means, and I don't. My father and my Uncle Al went into business together 23 years ago. On a hot tip from a friend of the family, they heard that the old man who owned The Ice Box was planning on retiring and that his burnt-out hippie son had no interest in continuing to oil the capitalist machinery. The old man's health was failing, faster since his wife had died the year before.

My father and my uncle knew a good deal when they saw one. They made this incredible-shrinking-man an offer he couldn't refuse, so he didn't. The Ice Box prospered as did my father and uncle. Then one day my mother looked at the calendar and realized that I was four years away from becoming a man. I remember my parents simultaneously slapping their foreheads and making an appointment with a rabbi.

The first three years of my religious education flew by like a pigeon wearing a ball and chain, and before we knew it, a hall had to be booked for the party. Caterers and florists and stationers had to be called. A tailor and a bandleader commissioned. A guest list had to be prepared. And so on.

Oh, the expense. After all, I was the oldest boy, and nothing was too good or too gaudy for me. And when it was all over, my parents were in over their heads. My father was forced to sell his share of the business. Had they known I would turn out to be an atheist and a homosexual, I suppose they would have proceeded at a slower, more reasonable pace. But they had witnessed other such functions, and while it is a solemn and reverential event, it is also something of a three-ring circus minus the dog act.

So now you and I know who's to bless and who's to be blamed for the fall of Communism, the confusion in what used to be Yugoslavia, the health care crisis, why there are no good roles for women in movies anymore, and the deficit (I mean my father's). Yours truly, Craig.

On that fateful evening in my parents' car, it dawned on me that bringing up the subject of moving back home, a subject I have wrestled with on and off for a year, was best saved for another time. As my imminent eviction and life on the street became ever more a reality, I began having this recurring nightmare where I'd taken up residency in the doorway of one or the other of those north Michigan Avenue multi-level indoor shopping malls.

In the nightmare my parents were a priest and a nun, leading a platoon of Salvation Army bell-ringers, handing out blessings and handfuls of cupcakes frosted the green of currency. They gave me one, which appeared smaller in my hands than in theirs. I gobbled it in one bite, and then in a voice like Mark Lester's in *Oliver!*, asked for another. My parents, the priest and nun, spun around to face me in their flowing tie-dyed robes and habit, and everything went silent with the exception of my request which echoed up and down the block.

Then, in a baritone I never knew she possessed, my mother broke into a song that would be considered a show-stopper in anyone's book. The Salvation Army bell-ringers spun around like dogs chasing their tails and became a chorus line of top-hat and tuxedoed tapdancers, the taps on their shoes sounding like quarters dropping onto Formica. My father, the dream-priest, picked me up by the ankles and began to shake me as thousands and thousands of nickels and dimes fell from the pockets of my homeless-person pants.

"Thought you could nickel and dime me to death, didn't you?" he roared and laughed, alternately shaking me and spinning me by the ankles like a figure skater. As the blood rushed through my ears, the sound of the tapping coins got louder and louder, sounding like hail gone berserk.

I awoke with a start. Sweat rolled down my forehead, nose, and chin. The sun through the windshield was so bright, I could barely open my eyes beyond a squint. There was sweat in my eyelashes. The tapping continued. I shielded my eyes with my left hand and looked out the driver's side window of the car.

There was this guy, my age or maybe younger, in a white t-shirt with a red ribbon silkscreened over his left pectoral. He was tapping on the window with a key and moving his mouth. His lips looked like the kind that women paid a small fortune in collagen injections and pain to obtain. Clean shaven, strong cleft chin, Roman nose, perfectly arched eyebrows. He was squinting, too, his Ray-Bans in his other hand, but I could make out his eyes a bluer shade of pale.

The slight lake breeze tousled his dark blond hair. He stopped talking and smiled to reveal two deep-end dimples. I was drowning in them, or was it my own perspiration? I leaned forward, my shirt peeling off the seat, making the sound that individually wrapped slices of American cheese made being unwrapped. The metal door crank was hot to the touch so I grasped it gently and opened the door slowly.

He was wearing short jean shorts, tight over his, dare I say bulging, thigh muscles. A runner, a body builder, a Roller-Blader? He crossed his arms in front of his chest and the muscles rippled like a mirage. He leaned forward, resting on the open door frame, into the inferno of the car.

"I'm having an acid flashback," I said, "and I don't even do acid."

"It'll pass," he said. "Just sit back."

He uncrossed his arms and eased me back against the seat. I jumped a little, my sweat-soaked shirt having had time to cool off.

"Easy," he said.

"Thanks, Conan," I said.

"Conan?" he asked. A puzzled puppy-dog look furrowed his tan brow.

"The barbarian," I said. "Those arms. You could probably carry me home without so much as a grunt of strain."

"That depends on where you live," Conan said and chuckled a he-man chuckle.

"In this car. I live in this car. I'd invite you in, but I apparently forgot to pay my electric bill."

"And fill the gas tank," Conan pointed to the empty fuel gauge.

He was right, of course. Aren't all mythological beings right?

"I have a gas can in the trunk of my car. If you want, I can take you to a gas station, and we can fill it up."

"Sure," I said, knowing full well that my pockets were empty, and my ATM card had been repossessed this morning. I wondered how Conan felt about running a tab. Suddenly the future didn't seem so dark as I stepped out into the sunlight of the breakdown lane.

MARILYN, MY MOTHER, MYSELF

Ever since I told my mother I was gay eight years ago, she had taken it upon herself to buy every Marilyn Monroe t-shirt, knickknack, poster, baseball cap, photograph (some autographed), calendar, greeting card, book, audio recording, videotape, engagement book, ceramic pin, button, Franklin Mint doll, and Bradford Exchange limited edition collector's plate she could get her hands on and present it to me.

"I saw this in the window at the Art Attack on Broadway," she'd say as she thrusted a square box wrapped in Marilyn-standing-over-the-subway-grating wrapping paper at my chest, "and couldn't remember if you had this or not."

"A Marilyn's-face ashtray. Thanks, Mom." I'd say, trying to sound like a kid on a commercial who had just been served a plate of his favorite macaroni and cheese shapes.

Still, I couldn't help but wonder whether or not a real fan might find flicking ashes and extinguishing lit cigarettes on Marilyn's birthmark or ruby red lips a bit objectionable or sacrilegious. At least she hadn't yet come across a Marilyn Monroe commemorative pillbox. That would have been too much, even for her.

Her quest, it seemed, was eternal. She ventured, on her own (my stepfather refused to be a party to her obsession), to parts of the city she never before knew existed, to find the missing pieces that would make my Marilyn collection complete. Dressing down and clutching her purse to her chest, she'd drive to the houses of other collectors living in the depths of the South Side, in Aurora, even as far west as Rockford, just so my already Marilyn-cluttered apartment could look more like a lost room at the Field Museum.

Each November 1st my mother tried unsuccessfully to conceal her disappointment when I told her that I'd attended yet another Halloween party not dressed as Marilyn Monroe. When I got a kitten and named it Tallulah, I sensed a strain in my mother's voice when we spoke on the phone or gathered for family functions and holidays during the following months.

I'd been toying with the idea of telling her that I was planning on leaving all of the Marilyn memorabilia to her in my will. Not that I was planning on dying anytime soon, but you never knew. Look at Marilyn, dead in the prime of her life.

Things could be worse, I supposed. What if she'd gone on a Judy Garland jag? Or leaned toward Liza Minelli? Barbra Streisand wouldn't have been half bad, but I'd already managed to cover that territory on my own.

I couldn't even get a typical tourist postcard from any of the exotic places my mother and stepfather visited since my stepfather's retirement. Somehow, my mother managed to find postcards in every foreign port she'd visited with pictures of Marilyn Monroe on them. I never knew Marilyn Monroe was so well traveled. But there she was, leaning out of a window, walking on a beach, eating a carrot in bed. Sending me greetings from Corfu, Belize, Tegucigalpa, Rio de Janeiro, Montevideo, Nice, and Samarkand.

On a domestic trip to Los Angeles to see my stepfather's younger brother and his third wife, my mother insisted on making her umpteenth visit to Marilyn's gravesite at Westwood for more snapshots. It was the 30th anniversary of her death, my mother exclaimed. How could she not pay her respects and shoot a roll of film for me, her only son, who was pining away for the tragic but legendary movie goddess?

The thing was, I wasn't even a fan of Marilyn Monroe's "body" of work. The only movie I'd ever seen with her in it was *All About Eve* (now Bette Davis is a different story altogether!), and I've been told it's one of Marilyn's early, smaller roles. Honestly, I couldn't tell *The Seven Year Itch* from a rash.

Just when I thought I'd reached the end of my frayed rope

and considered faking a pills and booze suicide in my parents' bed (Harold, from *Harold & Maude*, had more influence on me than Marilyn Monroe ever did, Mother, if you're paying attention), I came up with the next best thing. A Marilyn Monroe tattoo. Why not? Everyone else, from celebrities to nobodies, seemed to be doing it, so why shouldn't I? Besides, my mother hated tattoos. I think it had something to do with some of her relatives who had survived the Nazi concentration camps and had the numbers on their arms to show for it.

I, however, hated pain, and opted for a temporary tattoo. It was slightly more complicated than the lick-and-stick tattoos I used to get in boxes of Cracker Jack or from gumball machines, but I was certain that it would do the trick. The guy at the tattoo parlor guaranteed that it would last two weeks, through showers and saunas, hurricanes and tornadoes.

After the smiling-Marilyn-with-windblown-hair tattoo had been on my left bicep for a few days and the wrinkles had smoothed out, I invited my mother over for lunch. I used the excuse of wanting to show her how nicely her latest Marilyn "find" fit into the installation. She insisted on referring to my apartment as the "Norma Jean Shrine." I usually nodded my head in vague agreement.

I was wearing a muscle t-shirt that had been silkscreened with Marilyn in sunglasses and said PROVINCETOWN on it. For some reason, my mother stationed herself on my right side, when she came in and handed me her Indian blanket jacket which I hung on my Marilyn coat rack (a Home Consumer Network closeout). When we moved into the kitchen, laden with Marilyn potholders and trivets, aprons and coffee mugs, I positioned myself to her right and flexed my left arm.

Instead of swooning and asking for a cold compress for her forehead and a place to sit down, she oohed and aahed, as if she were having a private audience with the Hope Diamond.

"Cute! Just don't show your stepfather," she said in her most conspiratorial voice. "You know how he feels about tattoos!"

SWIMMING LESSONS

Neither of my parents could swim. That's why, they insisted, it was so important for me to learn how to swim. Swimming lessons, they said, the same way they said Sunday School or clean up your room. I agreed, swayed by their generosity. Their willingness to make me the best person I could be. Another set of lessons, another notch in my belt of accomplishments. Tapdancing lessons at the Art Linkletter Dance Studio, acting lessons with Mrs. DeWitt (the former Shakespearean actress), violin lessons with Mr. W at school. I even played Little League Baseball and Youth Basketball (one season of each), just so I and my parents could say I did it. Each one, an example of overachievement and excess. I could do anything, just not do it well.

Water sports snuck up on me late in life. By fourth grade, most of my contemporaries were already accomplished swimmers; bearers of Red Cross lifesaving certificates and patches. Whenever I went to the pool with my family (even though they couldn't swim, my parents found the public pool an excellent place to get sun and socialize), I remained at the shallow end, never getting into water I couldn't stand up in or walk in.

After dinner, one winter evening, my parents were watching *Hawaii Five-O*, eating popcorn and looking at a brochure from the Leaning Tower YMCA. I wondered if they were considering that pottery class that met on Tuesdays and Thursdays. The one in which my friend Jason was enrolled.

The way he talked about it, it sounded really cool. There were boxes of gray clay in cellophane that everyone took a handful from and put on their pottery wheel. Drawers full of special tools and jars of cloudy paints. Even an unusual oven, called a kiln, that reached extra high temperatures to bake each student's creation.

There was something in my parents' eyes as they huddled close together on the off-white couch, their legs entwined, the bowl of popcorn held between them, that told me they were investigating something a little less creative and a little more serious than throwing clay.

"Two weeks from Saturday," my father said, "you are going to begin swimming lessons." Usually they asked about the prospective lessons, giving me the chance to mull it over, or pretend to, and after giving the subject careful consideration, make time in my schedule of after school and weekend activities. They must have sensed my uneasiness in water and went ahead without my participation in the decision-making process and signed me up for swimming lessons.

As it turns out, my advanced drama lessons were coming to an end in a few weeks, and while I was hoping for voice lessons with Judith Lee at the Voice of Reason Vocal Conservatory, I was not surprised at my parents' action. And not really disappointed, either; because at some point the summer before, I realized two things. One was that I was missing out on a lot of fun. We took our first summer trip to Nippersink, a resort in Wisconsin where we would summer for the next ten years. Nippersink boasted one of the finest Olympic-size swimming pools in all of southern Wisconsin. While my parents were sunning and all the children my age were diving, racing and retrieving weighted rings off the bottom of the pool, I was befriending Carmen, the effervescent entertainment hostess.

I became her assistant, without pay as the recognition was enough. Putting the needle on the record when she gave group dance lessons, helping her supervise the decoration of the teen activity room (she valued my youthful opinion; she was pushing 60) and offering my attention with her wardrobe, which mostly consisted of low-cut one-piece bathing suits and kimonos.

The other thing I realized was that I loved to look at men. Not just men: teenagers and boys my age. While they were all turning their heads at whiplash speed every time a scantily clad female walked by, I couldn't keep my eyes off them. Suddenly, the way a voice begins to crack or dark curly hairs begins to appear between a belly button and a penis, I knew something was beginning that I couldn't stop.

By avoiding the pool and the locker room, I was missing out on the chance to see up close what I could only look at from a distance. How else could I see Steve Bernstein or Ricky Podowski, two of my favorite older kids, without shirts? I didn't go to the softball or volleyball games that seemed to be so popular with most of the boys and girls at Nippersink. I imagined that the minute they hit the playing field and felt the sun beating down on them, they took off their t-shirts and polo shirts, threw them in a pile near where the girls sat.

At the pool, there were no shirts, only solid and striped Speedos or baggy trunks. There were wide shoulders and brown nipples and tight skin. One night, during our week-long stay, I dreamt that I fell into the pool, that I struggled to stay above water in the deep end. One by one, the swimmers I admired from the balcony of the patio with one eye while I watched Carmen lead a group of great-grandparents through the Hokey Pokey with the other, dove into the pool to rescue me. Getting underneath me, lifting my limp, near-lifeless body up over their heads to carry me to the safety of the deck, where they took turns trying to revive me by administering the kiss of life. When I awoke, I was sitting up in the center of my bed, my summer pajamas on the floor with the pillow and top sheet. All the lights on in the suite, my parents looking at me with concern from their king-sized bed across the room.

On the Friday before the Saturday that my swimming lessons at the Y were to begin, my mother took me to S & M Sporting Goods downtown to buy a bathing suit. While we were there, I picked out nose clips, ear plugs and goggles. I hated buying a bathing suit because you couldn't try it on and you couldn't return it if it didn't fit. You had to hold it up against yourself and guess. I chose a pair of light blue trunks that I wouldn't feel too self-conscious wearing.

I wore the swim trunks under my corduroys that Saturday.

The other accessories were in an old gym bag my father found in the back of his closet which seemed to have been saved for such an occasion. My stomach felt queasy, and it hurt to breathe. I was sure I would drown during my first lesson, that no one would know how to save me, that my mother would have gone to the bathroom, stepped away for just a minute and come back to find me dead, floating face down in the water.

I was looking out the window, not paying attention to the passing scenery, when I saw the replica Leaning Tower go by and felt the car make that right turn into the driveway of the Y. I considered pleading with my mother, asking her to change her mind just this once, promising to do better at the next lesson, no matter what it was. I knew she would say no. "No," she'd say. "Besides, you've already worn the bathing suit, and we can't return it now."

The smell of chlorine that permeated the lobby of the Y had never bothered me before. Now it caused my eyes to water and squirmy stars to appear in the air. I staggered, dizzy and terrified, but my mother kept walking, with a mission, to the registration desk. I wondered if I could make myself faint, maybe hit my head on a piece of furniture, do something, anything to avoid getting into the pool.

I could see the pool through the gigantic picture window in the lobby. There were sofas and chairs arranged in front of the window so that parents could watch the lessons, beaming proudly at their water-borne offspring. I saw my mother put the latest James Michener novel in her bag before we left the house. She obviously had no desire to watch me floundering in the water. "Just give it your best effort," she said as she handed me the key-pin to my locker, the same thing she always said before a new set of lessons began. Then she pointed to a door that said MEN'S LOCKER ROOM and said, "March."

For the first few steps, I stumbled, then dragged my feet, then walked pigeon-toed. My mother cleared her throat, unimpressed with the display I had hoped would convince her of her and my father's grave and hasty mistake. So I marched, straight-backed and determined, into uncharted territory with my gym bag and a bad attitude.

The light in the locker room was brighter, more harsh, as if to make whatever lay on the other side of the door seem that much better. I walked past two rows of lockers, past the locker that my key-pin, #907, would unlock, to the two exits on the other end. One door had a plaque that said TRACK/COURTS. The other said POOL, and below that in smaller letters, CAUTION: WET SURFACE. I stood firmly rooted between the two doors, wondering if one of them had a secret emergency exit for situations like this one. A ladder perhaps, up the wall that led to a trap door in the ceiling and out onto the roof. I stepped forward, both arms outstretched toward both doors, when someone yelled, "Hey, you," and I dropped them to my sides like a soldier at attention.

Another voice asked, "What do you think you're doing?" I turned around to answer, curious to see who was asking the questions. For a moment I thought I was seeing double. Two skinny boys with gray sweatshirts and cuffed blue jeans, with gym bags over their shoulders. I closed one eye and looked. There were still two of them, blond hair almost white under the humming fluorescent tubes in the ceiling. They took a few steps toward me, and I stepped back. "Are you coming or going?" the one on the right asked. "Leaving or staying?" the one on the left asked.

"I haven't decided," I said. "Who wants to know?" That didn't sound as tough and self-assured as I wanted it to and regretted saying it instantly.

The twins looked at each other and shrugged. The one on the left said, "We were only asking because we know that Mr. Keith doesn't like anyone in the pool area with shoes on, and he'd probably start yelling and make you swim 20 laps or something."

"Twenty laps," I said. "Is that all?"

The one on the right walked over to a locker and opened it with his key-pin. He took his bag off his shoulder and put it on the bench behind him. He said something in a soft voice to the other one, and I realized that they knew I was bluffing. They looked to be about my age, maybe a year older. They sat down on the bench and began to undress. They took off their black Keds, left shoe first, then the right. They peeled off their white socks in the same order. I walked toward them and looked for my locker number at the same time. I wanted to say something to break the silence, but I didn't know what to say.

I found my locker about ten away from the twins. I put my gym bag down on a different bench and unzipped it. By then, they had already taken their sweatshirts off, and they were wearing bleached white t-shirts. And then they did something I couldn't believe. The one on the right pulled the t-shirt over the head of the one on the left and handed it to him. He hung it upon a hook in the locker and turned to the one on the right and did the same for him. He saw me watching and winked at me. I quickly looked away and began to undress, throwing my clothes into the locker.

When I looked at them again, they were adjusting their jockstraps and stepping into their bathing suits. I closed my locker and took my towel with me, trying to attach the key-pin to my trunks as I walked. Through the door marked POOL were the showers, hissing and steaming like prehistoric water snakes. I hung my towel on a hook and stood under the beating spray for a few seconds. As soon as I felt sufficiently damp, I got my towel and walked through the second door marked POOL.

At the shallow end of the pool, closest to the picture window, mothers were dropping infants in diapers and rubber pants into the water. They splashed, sank, and rose like bubbles. Giggling and slapping the water. The mothers wore bathing caps, some with flowers on them, their hair dry and invisible.

A group of kids, younger and older than I, was leaning against the wall under a hand-printed sign that said MINNOWS/BEGINNERS. I looked over at the picture window and saw my mother standing close to the glass, pointing in the direction of the wall and sign. "Over there," I mouthed, pointing, and walked slowly, cautious of the slippery tiles around the pool.

The clock on the opposite wall said 11:59. The lesson was supposed to begin at noon, and I decided to give the teacher until 12:01 to show up. After that I would meet my mother in the lobby and request that she demand a refund. At 11:59 and 57 seconds, the door from the men's locker room opened, and Paul, the instructor, walked through it.

He had thick brown hair, parted on the side that seemed to stay in place without Brylcreem, even after the showers. He wore a green racing suit, the same color as Robin's on *Batman*, but Paul filled out the front better. His skin was the color of clay pots and seemed like it would be warm if you touched it.

The part of his stomach above his belly button, which was an outie, reminded me of sand at the dunes after the wind blew it. Little peaks and valleys, ridges. Where his bathing suit ended, at the top of his thighs was a spill of brown hair which ran down to below his ankle bone and ended at his feet. The only other hair that color, besides on top of his head, was under his arms, which he raised above his head as he stretched.

"Okay, swimmers," he said. "Everybody into the pool." Everybody but me got into the water one way or another. Some sat on the edge of the pool and slid in. Others walked to where the ladders were and climbed down a step at a time. The braver ones jumped in, and it made me wonder if they knew more than they let on. Paul walked over to the wall where there was a clipboard among the life preservers, rubber toys, and kickboards.

Out of the corner of my eye, I could see the twins near the deep end of the pool by the diving boards. Apparently, they were more advanced swimmers. Learning how to dive or whatever it was that swimmers at their level did. I thought I saw one of them look over in my direction, but I couldn't be sure. Paul had begun to call roll from the list of names on the clipboard. He called mine, the last name on the sheet of paper and smiled at me. "Alright. Everybody pick a swim-mate. You," he said, looking into my eyes with eyes bluer than water, "will be mine."

YOUR MOTHER'S CAR

You are driving your mother's car. The blue 1980 Oldsmobile Cutlass station wagon. The one with fake wood panelling on the sides and back, and a luggage rack. There is a Snoopy air freshener hanging from the rearview mirror. Your baby shoes once hung in the same place.

This is the car the family took on cross-country trips. To the drive-in, where you and your brother always fell asleep in pajamas before the second feature began. You are driving your mother's car because your father ran over a skunk in his Camaro.

It is early summer, and you drive with all the windows down. It is night, the day after your birthday, and you hate air conditioning. Even at this hour the air is hot, oppressive. It is supposed to be cooler near the lake. You wonder how close you have to get.

The radio is playing good music. You have preprogrammed the buttons: a Top 40 station, an R & B station, an oldies station, and a college station. The last button is reserved for the Cubs game. The announcer's voice and the cheering crowd are a different kind of music. Background noise. The music stations are playing a lot of Sting. Phil Collins, too. You think Sting might be the most beautiful man in the world. You imagine that somewhere someone feels the same about Phil Collins.

You are driving your mother's car away from an ex-boyfriend's apartment. You are careful to say "ex-boyfriend," not "ex-lover," because you never really loved him. Besides, you were both so young, not quite men either. You like gray areas like that. But you felt an ache, like a toothache in your lap, when you saw him this time. The ache expanded when he hugged you and kissed you on the cheek.

Even in clothes, his body is better than you remembered. It must be the combination of dance and working out. Was he always this tall, you wonder? At least half-a-head taller than you and solid. Each curve, layer of muscle, defined under his shirt, like sculpture. You tell him how good he looks, each word sounding like you'd just relearned to speak after a stroke. Your heart is beating very fast. You can hear it in your ears.

Inside his apartment, you spend a few minutes catching up while you take small sips from the tall glass of ice water he brought you. The apartment is nicer than the last one he had. The neighborhood is not as nice, but he insists it is one of the up-and-coming parts of the city.

Outside, you hear the heavy metal rumble of the el pulling into the Bryn Mawr station, sirens, breaking glass. For a moment you wonder if your mother's car is all right, parked on the street.

Since you've both already eaten dinner, he suggests going out for a drink. You aren't a big drinker, but you agree anyway. So many new bars have opened since you moved away. He suggests Different Strokes, the bar where he works a few nights a week.

It was there that you tracked him down after a mutual friend mentioned seeing him tending bar. You surprised him while he was pouring a drink for a customer. He came out from behind the bar to see you closer, the look of disbelief on his face like a mask. He hugged you, and you hugged him back, surprised that he was so glad to see you after all you put him through. In one scenario you had imagined him stabbing you with a corkscrew.

In the hallway he triple-locks the door to his apartment from the outside. He mentions something about a police lock, then changes the subject. Out in front of the building the street is suddenly quiet as if the neighborhood had fallen into a deep, drugged sleep.

You unlock the passenger's door of your mother's car for him. He gets in and leans across the seat to unlock your door. While you are putting your seatbelt on, you feel him staring at you. When you look over at him, he smiles and kisses you on the cheek. He tells you how much he likes you without a beard.

You pull your mother's car out of the parking space, and it is filled by a car you would swear appeared out of nowhere. When you get to Clark Street, he tells you to turn right. On the way you pass a bar called the Gold Coast. You can remember when the Gold Coast used to be on the downtown end of Clark Street, not this far north. How one night, before you moved away, you and some friends agreed to hit some Chicago nightlife landmarks as your last group outing.

You remember how dark the bar was except for dim lights behind the bar. You remember circular movement, like the men in the sanitarium scene in *Midnight Express*, moving in the same direction around a pillar. Anyone going against the flow was pushed, forced to join the current. You felt dizzy, deprived of light and air. You lost your friends, and panic rose in your throat like bile.

When you were about to abandon hope, one of them appeared at your side, grabbed you by the hand, and led you down some stairs where the light was colored, but better. From the third or fourth step down, you could see what looked like jail cells. You broke away from your friend's grip, tripped up the stairs and out the door. Waiting for your friends to come out of the bar, you were propositioned more times than you cared to count. Some offered money.

You park your mother's car a few doors away from the new Gold Coast after he suggests stopping in there first since you're so close. It's different now, he assures you; less scary. Besides a friend of his is a bartender there and you can drink for free. The hardcore scene has changed, he tells you with what you think is a knowing look. You wonder how much as two men in leather chaps and harnesses hold the door open for you.

He is right. The first thing you notice is how much better lit it is inside. Almost bright. There is a large color TV hanging from leather straps and silver chains over the bar. The men at the bar are mesmerized by the action on the screen. You assume they are watching pornography. It turns out to be *The Marva Collins Story* with Cicely Tyson.

As you get closer to the bar, you notice a man in faded Levi's and tank shirt, wiping his damp eyes with a yellow bandanna.

You both sit on stools at the bar and order your drinks in a whisper, so as not to disturb the other patrons.

His bartender friend isn't working, so he pays for the first round of drinks. You take your club soda and follow him to another part of the bar, a room where a Harley-Davidson is parked in the middle of the floor. Your conversation is animated.

You sense that he is trying to prove how well he's done without you. You want to tell him not to try so hard. He doesn't have to impress you. You still like him; knew that he'd make it. He never gets angry, only remorseful, and his voice gets all scratchy and soft. You wonder what he saw in you; try to remember what you didn't see in him.

You are on the rebound from a relationship that ended, like a song, after four years. He has had numerous lovers, none serious enough to last. After the next round of drinks, you suggest moving on to another bar. The Gold Coast has filled up since you arrived, and you brush past several fierce-looking men on the way out. You try to avoid looking directly into their eyes.

The weather has changed while you were in the bar. The heat, risen, uncovers a layer of cool air that feels like a splash of water in the face. You are glad that you brought that old high school letter jacket that your older brother gave you. You put it on inside the car, and he laughs. You met at that school, and he says that he doesn't remember you being on any athletic team. You tell him that you were the tiddlywink champion of the school, and you both laugh.

Halfway to the next bar he asks you if you would mind taking him home, instead. He is feeling very tired all of a sudden, and he has to be at rehearsal early the next morning for a show he is choreographing. You tell him you understand. You forget that just because you are on vacation and can stay out all night, not everyone is that lucky.

On the way to his apartment, you think about saying good night in your mother's car. You want to avoid walking him to his door. You wonder if you would sleep with him if he asked you. You wonder if he will ask you.

You turn your mother's car onto his street. There is nowhere to park in front of his building. You drive around the block once without any luck. You double-park in front of his building. You both get out of the car, which you leave running, and embrace. A car pulls up behind you and honks. You are secretly grateful. You say good night.

You are driving your mother's car north on Clark Street. You have a reasonably good arrangement regarding transportation with your parents. There is almost always a car available for you to drive, when you come home to visit for a few weeks every summer. You know it is very considerate of them to make sure there is a car at your disposal.

Sometimes there is a catch. Like tonight, for example. You can stay out as late as you like just as long as your mother has the car back in time to get to her Early-Bird-Aerobics class at 7:15 the next morning. You are proud of her for staying in such good physical condition. She has run in six 10K races. She is probably in better shape than you are. This doesn't bother you; only makes you think that she will probably outlive you.

You change the stations on the radio, as you consider which route to take home. Once you read somewhere that it is a good idea to vary your patterns, especially the direction you take going home. You have so many choices; you are almost dizzy with indecision.

There is any number of streets, heavily trafficked or residential that you can take. You stay on Clark Street for a few blocks. There is no need to rush into a decision. You could even pull over for a few minutes and think about it. You check your watch. It is only 11:30.

At the next stoplight, you are the first car in the left lane. A light blue Honda Accord pulls up next to your mother's car. You are singing along with the radio. "Road to Nowhere" by Talking Heads. You suddenly feel self-conscious, your singing off-key with all the windows down. You push the buttons, and the back windows go up automatically.

You notice the driver of the Honda looking at you, smiling. You meet his eyes, still singing. He is very handsome; gorgeous, really. The streetlights illuminate the inside of his car as if he had turned on the interior light. Dark hair and a mustache. Very tan. If the light was just a little better, you could make out the color of his eyes. Right now the color is insignificant. What matters is that he hasn't stopped looking at you.

The light changes to green, and your foot is on the gas pedal, like reflex. You both manage to keep up, driving next to each other. At the next stoplight he is still next to you. Your hands are squeezing the steering wheel so tightly you have cut off the circulation to your fingertips. You know that if you loosen your grip, your hands will do a spasmodic dance, float above your head in an explosion of nerves.

On the beige vinyl seat, next to your right thigh, is a pack of Marlboro Lights. You pry your right hand off the steering wheel and let it fall onto the seat. You flip the box-top open and extract a cigarette. It takes a few seconds to decide whether to use the car's lighter or the Bic disposable. You push the lighter into the dashboard and light the cigarette with the Bic.

You lock eyes with him again, and the light changes. You cross the intersection in what feels like slow motion. The lighter on the dashboard clicks and startles you. He takes the lead as you drop back. Another car behind his tries to pass you. You let it as he pulls in front of you.

There is a cloud of smoke in his car as he lights a cigarette. You take this as a good sign: you have something in common. He is looking in his rearview mirror, making sure you are still there. You look in your rearview mirror to double-check.

After you both cross Devon Avenue, the traffic merges into one lane. You stay close behind him, but not too close in case you have to make a sudden stop. You are surprised at how rationally you are behaving. After all, you think, nothing could come of this.

Your shoulders are tense, and you realize that you are practically hunched over the steering wheel, a position you find yourself in when you are driving in a particularly bad rainstorm. You force yourself to sit back, press your shoulders into the vinyl seat-back. You alternately flick cigarette ashes out the window and into the ashtray. You will have to remember to clean out the ashtray before putting the car in the garage. Your mother has told you on more than one occasion how she feels about your smoking. You toss the cigarette out the window, which misses the window of an oncoming car.

There is a lot of traffic on the street for a weeknight. There is a bar on every corner in this neighborhood; people spilling out of the entrances and onto the sidewalks. You think about pulling up next to the Honda at the next stoplight, taking the lead in this game.

Your mind is in a million places at once: listening to the radio, looking out for pedestrians, trying to light another cigarette, following the blue Honda. He runs a yellow light, leaving you behind as it changes to red. Your heart sinks like an anchor until you see him pull over halfway down the block.

The light turns green, and you are next to him in what seems like light-speed. He motions for you to take the lead. He is right behind you, following closer than you did. You wonder if he thinks you are going to take him back to your house.

You imagine sneaking him in, up the stairs, past your parents' bedroom, where they sleep unaware on their king-sized brass bed. Into the bedroom you used to share with your older brother before he got married. You imagine undressing him in the dark, moving slowly, locked in an embrace, to the bed, where your parents' pit bull terrier Cerberus sleeps when you're not around. You decide to let him resume the lead at the next stoplight.

For a few blocks on Clark Street, there are no parked cars, and he pulls up next to you and smiles. Perfect white teeth, a dimple in his right cheek, and blue eyes. He is listening to the same radio station as you. Whitney Houston whines "Saving All My Love for You." You take your foot off the gas pedal, slow down without braking, and he automatically takes the lead. You are approaching Howard Street.

When you get to the other side of Howard Street, Clark Street will become Chicago Avenue, and you will be in Evanston. You decide not to follow him any further than Main Street, which is less than a mile from where you are presently. Your parents' house is off Main Street, and you could lose him easily if you needed to. But now you are following him.

As your self-imposed boundary gets closer, you consider extending it for a few more blocks. You speed up at the last minute and pass him as he turns left two blocks before Main Street. The block before Main Street is one way in the other direction. You turn left onto Main Street as the stoplight changes to red. You imagine being pulled over by an irate, bored cop, explaining to him that you are in hot pursuit of the man of your dreams, would he mind waiting a few minutes, you'd be right back.

You look in your rearview mirror, find no flashing lights behind you, not even another car. You drive down two blocks and turn onto the street you are sure you saw the blue Honda turn. He is waiting for you at the stop sign on the corner.

Now that you are off the busy city streets and on the quiet Evanston neighborhood streets, you begin to have serious second thoughts. He turns right, then left into an alley. You drive to the end of the next block and stop at the corner. One of the radio stations is signing off for the night. You look at your watch; it is 12:00. You give yourself 15 minutes to decide what to do.

The progressive radio station is playing something by Husker Dü. The grinding guitars are strangely soothing. You turn right, then right again at the next corner. You drive around the block, repeating the same turns. A man is standing in front of a large, old apartment building. You drive past slowly and his head turns, following your mother's car down the block.

At the corner you make another right turn, then an immediate right into the alley you saw the Honda turn down. There is a parking lot behind the big, old apartment building, and you see the blue Honda in one of the white gravel spaces. You lightly honk the horn as you approach the sidewalk-end of the alley. He is standing on the corner under a streetlamp. There is something vaguely cinematic about this as you pull your mother's car up closer to him.

He is wearing a white t-shirt and black jeans. He takes one last drag from a cigarette and tosses it into the street. He is walking toward you, and you can see that he is wearing white Reeboks like your mother wears to her Early-Bird-Aerobics class. You turn off the radio; you can't hear it anyway.

The blood is pounding in your ears, making them ring and burn simultaneously. He is walking toward your mother's car, with you in the driver's seat, smiling as brightly as the chrome on the bumpers when the car was new. You smile, too, as you reach across the driver's seat of your mother's car to unlock the door on the passenger's side.

He opens the door and slides into the front seat of your mother's car. His eyes are as blue as the paint on your mother's car. You want to climb inside of them and take them for a test drive. You know nothing will ever be the same. Not you, not your mother's car.

ABOUT THE AUTHOR

Gregg Shapiro's poetry collection *Protection* was published by Gival Press in 2008, and his 2012 chapbook *GREGG SHAPIRO: 77* was published by Souvenir Spoon Books. His poetry and fiction have appeared in numerous outlets including literary journals such as *BAC Street Journal, Beltway Poetry Quarterly, BLOOM, Court Green, Gargoyle, Jonathan, Mary: A Literary Quarterly, Pearl, RHINO Poetry*, and *White Crane Journal*. He has also appeared in the anthologies *Among the Leaves: Queer Male Poets on the Midwestern Experience* (Squares & Rebels), *Best Gay Poetry 2008* (Lethe Press), *Blood to Remember* (Time Being Books), *Collective Brightness: LGBTIQ Poets on Faith, Religion & Spirituality* (Sibling Rivalry Press), *Encounters: Poems about Race, Ethnicity and Identity* (Skinner House Books), *Full Moon on K Street* (Plan B Press), *Hibernation and Other Poems by Bear Bards* (Bear Bones Books), *Mondo Barbie* (St. Martin's Press), *Reclaiming the Heartland* (University of Minnesota Press), *Sex & Chocolate: Tasty Morsels for Mind and Body* (Paycock Press), *Unsettling American* (Penguin), and *Windy City Queer* (University of Wisconsin Press). His often-anthologized poem "Tattoo" can be found in numerous textbooks. As an entertainment journalist, he writes interviews and reviews for a variety of regional LGBT publications and websites. A Chicago native, Shapiro has also lived in Boston and Washington, D.C. He currently resides in Fort Lauderdale, Florida with his husband Rick and their dog k.d.

www.ingramcontent.com/pod-product-compliance
Lightning Source LLC
Chambersburg PA
CBHW060335260626
47160CB00007B/2800